Only Option

The Only Option
By Megan Derr

Published by Megan Derr

Edited by Samantha M. Derr
Cover designed by Michelle Seaver

Second Edition July 2017
First published May 2016 by All Romance Ebooks

Printed in the United States of America

The ONLY OPTION

Megan Derr

CHAPTER ONE

Rochus pulled off his spectacles and wiped them clean as the door of the tavern slammed shut behind him. Noise washed over him, along with the smell of cheap food and too many unwashed people, an undercurrent of smoke, and the faint tingle of magic. He stared through the large, open archway into the dining hall, the need for food warring with a need for solitude and a reluctance to endure the stares that would come when everyone realized what he was.

But he detested hiding in his room like he was something to be ashamed of, and hiding wouldn't stop the rumors or whispers. So he slipped his spectacles back on and approached the counter, pushing back the hood of his cloak. He set two worn, gleaming coins on the counter, ignoring the wide eyes and gaping mouth of the man behind it. "A room, a bath, supper, and breakfast."

"Supper and—" The man snapped his mouth shut. "Of course, magus. Um…" He picked up the coins, eyes flitting about nervously. So close to the royal castle, one would think they'd be more used to the likes of Rochus, but then again, most of his kind preferred to avoid undue attention, and the rest were spoiled brats who'd never settle at a cheap tavern when the royal castle was only a few more hours away.

Stifling a sigh, Rochus answered the question the man couldn't quite get out. "Pig or cow blood will work fine, and chicken or some other fowl if that's the best you can muster. A full pitcher of it, though merely a cup will suffice if more cannot be found. Not horse." They were far too expensive to drain, and the taste wasn't worth it.

"Y-yes, magus. Um." The man licked his lips. "Will you want to see the room first or go straight to the dining hall?"

"The room, and I'll take the bath after I've dined."

The man murmured another affirmative, tucked the coins away, and slid a key across the counter. "Up the stairs, all the way at the very end of that first hall."

"My thanks," Rochus replied and resettled his saddlebags on his shoulder before heading up the dark, creaky steps and down the long hallway. It branched off in three places, but as promised, his was the room at the very back of the first, main hallway.

It smelled of dust and disuse, with a slight tingling-tang of old, faded magic. Powerful magic, likely wards or some other cage meant to keep something in. But the inn had once been a castle in its own right, before it had been torn down and rebuilt, changed to something less expensive and more profitable than an empty fortress. It wasn't surprising remnants of the fortress remained in more than the old stones.

He dropped his saddlebags on the bed and

quickly sent his heavy travel cloak after them. Removing his spectacles, he combed fingers through his short, sweat-damp hair. In the dark room, with nothing but slips of moonlight to lend visibility, his hair appeared black. Better lighting would prove it to be blue, so too his nails and teeth. It was the teeth that always made people most uncomfortable — dark blue, some more pointed than they should be, all the more stark against his too-white skin.

Rochus briefly considered changing into fresh clothes, but there was little point until after he'd had a bath — and no telling what would happen in the dining hall. It would hardly be the first time some country bumpkins or foreign nitwits wailed superstitious nonsense and tried to kill him, nevermind he reported directly to the crown.

He smoothed out his robes, frowning at a small tear in the right sleeve. He'd have to stitch it later after his bath.

For the moment, it was time for supper, and hopefully he'd get to enjoy it in peace.

Heading back downstairs, Rochus walked into and through the dining hall, keeping his head up even when the whispers started.

Necromancer.

Half-dead.

Blood-drinker.

His lips curled briefly when he heard someone ask their companion if Rochus was a vampire. As though he was one of those needle-teethed, full-dead mongrels. He drank blood and his teeth were meant for hunting, but it wasn't the same

thing. His teeth were more like those of a wolf —
teeth he did not use thus because he was a
civilized, capable necromancer of forty-three, not
some ravening monster.

Rochus sat down at a table in the corner where
he wasn't too close to the fire but would still be
warm and would be able to see anyone who tried
to approach him.

A couple of minutes after he sat, a pale-faced
young man brought him a pitcher and cup with
faintly trembling hands. Rochus slid a coin across
the table, nodding for him to take it. The boy took
it and skittered away, and the whispers increased
as Rochus poured himself a cup of blood and
sipped it. Pig, which he preferred, save for those
rare occasions he was able to get something as
decadent as human.

He took several more sips, savored the way it
warmed him through. There was nothing he
hated more than being cold, but it was the one
thing he would always be due to what was called
his half-dead state. He wasn't actually dead, half
or otherwise, but necromancy demanded a high
price, drained away half his spirit, replaced it with
those unique spiritual energies he needed to wield
his strange magic. The physical effects — the
corpse white skin, the death-black bones, the need
for food replaced by a need for blood — were what
earned necromancers the reputation of being half-
dead.

But many a threat came from death, and only
those who could manipulate death stood any
chance against them, and so every generation, lots

were drawn from the newest magi and the chosen became necromancers.

He sipped more blood as he kept one eye on the restless, whispering crowd. They didn't feel dangerous, but that undercurrent of tingling magic remained, which made him nervous. Though all magic started the same, and it was pure chance who would become a necromancer, still they were set apart—because of their power, their reputation, their *otherness*. Where necromancers walked, they most often walked alone. Even family usually backed away. Rochus had always been grateful his family was not so fragile, that he was not the reason his mother had moved far away; that instead she was happily wreaking havoc while his stepfather looked on with adoration and amusement.

Turning away from the crowds, he pulled out the small book hidden in the folds of his robes and opened it to the marked page. The faded letters were hard to read in the flickering firelight, but it was a book he'd read numerous times; he knew the words even when he couldn't read them. Removing his glasses, he settled into reading, a whisper-soft smile curving his lips.

He'd just refilled his cup and resumed reading when a discreet cough interrupted his solitude. Dragging his eyes from his book, Rochus looked up—and froze. A dragon. There was no mistaking those banked-coal eyes, the faintly sweet, smoky scent of dragonfire that surrounded him. He was also young, mid-twenties or so. His light brown skin was covered in freckles, especially over the broad, slightly flat nose. The hair was a touch overlong, the stiff, springy curls tousled like he ran his hands through them frequently. It looked dark brown, but Rochus would be willing to bet there were hints of red in it.

Strangely, the dragon was plainly dressed. There wasn't anything even remotely shiny anywhere on his clothes—no jewels, gold, silver, not even polished wood or bone. Rochus had never met a dragon that didn't try to wear half their hoard, but he supposed there was a first time for everything. "What do you want, kit?"

"I'm not a kit," the dragon replied, mouth curving. "I'm more than old enough to know my mind and go about getting what I want."

"If you're hoping for a fight, I suggest you try the drunks in the opposite corner. They seem that particular type of bloodthirsty. My bloodthirst is much more mundane."

"I'm not one for fighting," the dragon said and helped himself to an empty chair, pulling it over to Rochus's table and sitting so close he may as well have been in Rochus's lap. He smelled even better up close, earthy and smoky and *warm*. But he was half Rochus's age if he was a day, so whatever the reason for the clumsy flirting, it wasn't actually about flirting.

Rochus hadn't been that lucky when he'd been younger and still good looking enough his strange appearance made him exotic to some. Nowadays he was merely strange on a good day, creepy on most, terrifying on the worst.

The dragon's fingers rested on his arm as he

leaned even further into Rochus's space. "What's your name, magus?"

"Try giving yours first," Rochus replied, tucking his book away and shoving his spectacles back in place. "Brazen I will tolerate. Rude I will not."

Laughing, the dragon replied, "Fair enough, my apologies. I'm Tilo Landau of Rothenberg Kill." He touched the center of his forehead and dipped his head. "Honor to make your acquaintance, magus."

Rochus touched his forehead. "I doubt it's much of an honor. Magus Rochus Kraemer. What do you want, kit?"

The hand still resting on his arm tightened, and Tilo leaned in close enough that his lips brushed Rochus's ear as he said, "Things that wouldn't interest little kits."

Rochus jerked away. "I sincerely doubt that. If you are hoping to lure me away so you and your friends can beat me and set me aflame, you are toying with the wrong necromancer." He'd fallen for that once, only once, and spent weeks recovering from the mistake. The shame and humiliation—those had taken years to overcome. "Leave me in peace or you will regret it."

"No game," Tilo replied. "I've been searching for someone interesting all night, was about to give up and take care of matters alone. Then you walked in."

Rochus snorted and drank a deep swallow of blood, hoping it would remind Tilo exactly what he was talking to and drive him away. But if he noticed or cared, Tilo made no sign of it. "I'm not so old I'm feeble or gullible, kit. You are not very good at coaxing men into alleyways, whatever your motives. You are half my age if you are a day; I find it hard to believe I am the only interesting prospect this room has to offer. Go find someone your own age to fuck and leave me to my reading."

In reply, Tilo grabbed the back of Rochus's neck, turned his head, and kissed him hard. But it wasn't the kiss that was immediately distracting — it was the sweet smoke and hot metal taste of dragon blood. The little brat had bitten his own lip. Rochus had never tasted anything like it. The warm pig blood was ice cold by comparison. Tilo's blood left him feeling like he was filled with boiling water; it banished the inescapable cold like fire melting ice. Rochus gasped, tried to pull away, but Tilo seemed to take his reaction as permission and kissed him harder, shifting closer so the long lines of his body pressed against Rochus's side. He wasn't just warm, he was hot, even through all the layers of cloth between them.

Rochus managed to get his mouth free, but somehow, instead of pulling free entirely, he just wound up with a lapful of dragon, his spectacles gone, and two hands buried in his hair. That mouth dropped right back on his, hot and wet and greedy, plundering like a mercenary come upon a forgotten tomb full of untold riches.

So far as convincing Rochus to do something stupid, it was a much more effective method than Tilo's previous efforts. Despite himself, Rochus responded, curling an arm around Tilo's waist, fisting the other hand in those lovely curls, holding Tilo still while he showed the little brat how it was done. He slowed the kiss, gentled it, tongue exploring Tilo's mouth in leisurely strokes and sweeps. He didn't relent until Tilo was trembling in his arms, and then only because he didn't like to make more of a spectacle of himself than necessary and this had gotten quite out of hand.

Tilo licked his lips, eyes no longer banked coals but a blazing fire. "Shall we take this upstairs?" He rolled his hips, grinding the hard length of his trapped cock against Rochus's. "I promise all I want to do is fuck you."

"After that display, I've little choice but to depart else the innkeeper will throw us both out," Rochus replied and let Tilo pull him to his feet. He paused only to snatch up his discarded spectacles, and tucked them away in his robes as he followed Tilo out of the dining room.

Rochus paid the stares and whispers even less attention leaving than he had arriving, more distracted than he liked admitting by the warm hand clinging to his as he led the way up to his room. They were barely inside when Tilo pushed him against the door and practically climbed him. If Rochus had thought the kisses in the dining hall were impressive, they had nothing at all on the way Tilo devoured his mouth then, plundering it like he intended to take Rochus for his hoard, keep him locked up and ever-ready to be used when and how Tilo saw fit. Rochus shivered, arms tightening around Tilo as he met the fevered kiss full measure.

He still suspected Tilo's motives, but for the moment he wasn't going to complain if some young, fiery, pretty little dragon wanted to fuck him. With an effort, he pulled away just enough to say, "There's a bed, kit."

"Stop calling me kit," Tilo muttered between more kisses, but he slid down Rochus's body and walked backward toward the bed, stripping off his clothes as he went.

Tilo was even more beautiful naked, lean and long, light brown skin golden in the light of the fire someone had laid when they'd delivered the bathtub and hot water set in front of it. He perched on the edge of the bed and spread his legs, resting his hands on his thighs, baring everything for Rochus's hungry perusal. "Let's see you now, magus."

Rochus double-checked the door was locked, then tugged the laces at the throat of his dark blue robe. In the warmer seasons, it was all he wore over a pair of breeches and high boots. In winter, he wore wool skirts beneath, visible through the open sides of the robe.

Discarding it, he sent the skirt and underclothes quickly following. His cock was harder than he could remember it being for longer than he cared to think about. He stroked it leisurely as he walked to the bed, where Tilo still sat, body still but his eyes vibrant with want. Tilo reached out and tangled his fingers with Rochus's around his cock, hand so hot it felt like fire.

Rochus sucked in air, unable to breathe for a moment, shuddering as that heat rushed through him.

Tilo made a soft, growly little noise and then Rochus was being dragged onto the bed and stretched out across it. Tilo spread across his thighs and bent to put that impertinent little mouth to work, dragging a rough tongue and sharp teeth across Rochus's skin, chasing the stings with wet, sucking kisses.

Rochus wasn't used to being so overwhelmed he couldn't think, but he gave up the struggle with little hesitation, far too intoxicated by the heat and focus consuming him to care about what might come after. He twined his fingers in Tilo's hair and dragged him up to get another taste of that mouth, sucking on Tilo's tongue, pressing his own deep to taste every curve and crevice. Tilo fed more of those hungry growls to him, along with ragged moans and a few greedy demands Rochus was happy to oblige.

Getting his other arm around Tilo's lithe frame, Rochus flipped them over, got a grip on Tilo's wrists, and did some devouring of his own. His skin was soft, so hot to the touch it burned away any level-headed thoughts that might have remained. Rochus wanted to sink into that heat and stay there for hours. Days. So long he would never feel cold again.

"You should bite me," Tilo bit out in ragged gasps, bucking up against Rochus, rubbing his hard, leaking cock against Rochus's skin and leaving trails of fire. "Bite me as you fuck me, necromancer."

Rochus shuddered, let go of one of Tilo's wrists to grab his own cock to keep himself from coming.

Tilo chuckled, low and husky. "Thought you'd like that idea. Fresh blood with the pulse still going, you light up like a dragon with a chest of jewels, hmm."

"Your mouth," Rochus said and bit off Tilo's laugh with another wet, toothy kiss that left them both gasping.

"Jacket," Tilo said. "My jacket has something useful in them."

Rochus's mouth twitched with a faint smile as he withdrew and fetched Tilo's jacket, quickly found the little bottle of bedroom oil there. "You were on a particular quest tonight, weren't you?" He spread Tilo's thighs furthers apart and teased his hole with two slick fingers. "That's right," he murmured as Tilo clung to him, shivered against him, eyes bright and hot with need. "Tremble for me, little dragon. Beg me for it."

"Fuck me, magus. I've waited long enough." He broke off with a hard shudder and a gasped curse as Rochus shoved a finger inside him, but by the time Rochus had worked in a second, he was back to giving orders. Rochus nipped at his throat, left a line of marks along the long line of it as he worked three fingers into that tight heat. Oh, to drag the torment out all night, see what it took to make his little dragon howl and scream.

He shook that thought aside, banished it to join all the other unwanted thoughts that had burned away. Withdrawing his fingers, he slicked his cock and pressed it to Tilo's hole, then once more captured those slender wrists and pressed them firmly to the bedding. He bit hard at Tilo's throat as he pushed inside his body, felt the deep moan that drew out.

"Rochus—" Tilo struggled against his grip, but not with any real effort. If he'd been trying, a dragon at full strength could toss Rochus clear across the room and, if angry enough, through the wall. He growled. "Fuck me, already."

Rochus pulled out slightly and then slammed back in, stilling again as Tilo moaned even louder, then repeated the motion, stilling every time until Tilo finally howled for him, long and broken and desperate. Only then did Rochus give him the hard pounding they both craved, going until he could scarcely breathe and his entire body ached with it, trembled with the effort of holding off his own climax.

When he could take no more, he bent and sank his teeth into Tilo's throat, this time breaking skin, filling his mouth with the hot, sweet taste of fresh dragon blood as he slammed into Tilo's body one last time and came apart. Tilo screamed as he came, his release hot and sticky between them.

Rochus slumped atop him until he could muster the energy to roll off. He turned on his side to face the door, yawning as exhaustion followed quickly in the wake of several days of hard travel followed by an unexpectedly busy evening.

Behind him, Tilo had already dropped off, snoring softly, one arm draped lazily over

Rochus's hips. Normally Rochus would wake him up and tell him to go, but he was entirely too lethargic to muster the energy. Against all sense, he let sleep overtake him.

He was stirred in the night by a mouth on his throat and slick, clever fingers returning all the teasing torment Rochus had subjected Tilo to earlier. Sleepiness warred with desire, and Rochus reached up a heavy, fumbling hand to drag Tilo closer, turning to kiss him awkwardly. "Get on with it then, kit."

A husky chuckle filled Rochus's ear and then the fingers withdrew, quickly followed by a long, hard cock that wasted no time in fucking Rochus into sharp, hungry wakefulness. After a few firm thrusts, however, Tilo withdrew. Before Rochus could begin lobbing curses at him, he rolled Rochus to his stomach and up onto his knees, then spread him wide and fucked back into him, pounding with hard, deep strokes that left Rochus breathless and dizzy.

The hazy, dim-lit world around them vanished entirely as he came apart a second time, gasping for breath, then moaning as Tilo pressed his wrist to Rochus's mouth and filled it with sweet blood once more.

By the time Rochus once more stretched out on the bed, he could barely breathe, let alone think or, goddess forbid, move. He only barely felt the soft brush of lips against his cheek, barely heard the softly murmured, "Farewell, magus," and the quiet opening and closing of the door.

He woke to gray, hazy sunlight and a familiar

rough tongue on his cheek. Groaning, Rochus cracked open one eye and glared blearily. "Memory. Can't you ever let a man sleep?" Hadn't the door been closed? Well, that rarely did more than slow Memory down.

Memory purred at him and gently butted her head against his cheek. Rochus sighed and sat up, folding his legs in front of him and smiling faintly as Memory climbed into his lap for her morning petting. She was the very color of white-gray mist, long-haired, fluffy, and enormous—what was known as a Valder Mountain Cat.

She was also dead. She'd been the runt of the litter, too small and weak to survive, and had died within minutes of being born. Normally bringing the dead back to half-life was impossible, for the only way to do it was in the immediate moments following death, when the spirit was still within and there were sufficient dregs of life to be filled with necromantic power. But he'd been there when she'd breathed her last and surrendered to an impulse, filling her with his power. She'd been his faithful companion ever since. Though Song, Silence, and Fury were also dear to him, Memory was most precious.

"Yes, I'm aware I smell funny," he said when she mewed at him and pricked his skin slightly. "You'll have to get over it because I'm not remotely sorry." The only thing he was sorry about was not being able to enjoy a morning farewell, but given the night's performance, he doubted he'd have been capable of it anyway.

That being said, he could not remember the

last time he'd felt so invigorated. Tilo's blood was like nothing he'd ever had. Or was likely to have again, since Tilo was the only dragon in his forty-three years who'd offered him blood. Until then, the finest thing Rochus had ever tasted was the blood of a healer, and that had been given with great reluctance. No one had ever offered it up so willingly — so eagerly.

"Best not to waste it then," he murmured, and after a few last pettings, lifted Memory off his lap and set her aside. "You're in a good mood this morning. Catch yourself a nice plump bird to feast upon?" Memory meowed and preened, and Rochus smiled as he climbed out of bed and went to bathe in the long-cooled water.

When he was clean and dressed in fresh clothes, and his belongings were packed away, he lifted Memory up and settled her in the crook of one arm, his saddlebags slung over the other shoulder. "Come on, then. The sooner this is over with, the sooner we can all be home again."

Not that he was in a particular hurry to know why the queen was summoning him to the royal castle. Usually when she had work for him she sent a clerk with all the necessary information and payment. The one and only time he'd had to go to the castle for an assignment was when he was fresh out of training and they wanted a look at him before trusting him to act in the crown's name.

Hopefully the task would not be too onerous, but he wasn't counting on it. Any problem requiring a necromancer was already nearly as bad as it could get, and any problem requiring he first speak directly to the queen...

Well, he'd almost rather be a damned vampire.

Outside, he walked through the chilly, faintly misty air to the stable across the yard and handed over a pence to the boy who'd watched his unicorn for him in the night. Though Fury was missing his horn, sawed off long ago by poachers who'd left him for dead, he was still as beautiful and lively as any unicorn Rochus had ever met. At least he had been once he'd healed up, which had taken time, not least of all because keeping things alive was not a skill Rochus had ever been required to learn.

Fury's coat and hair were the color of pitch, with a faint rainbow luster to it in full daylight. The stump of his horn gleamed like a black pearl, and his eyes were a swirling, jewel-bright green. He whinnied softly as Rochus approached.

"Good morning, my handsome fellow," Rochus murmured, stroking Fury's velvety nose. "Were you treated well?" That got him nuzzled, and Rochus smiled. "Good." He led Fury out of his stall and got him ready, then led him into the yard. Rochus swung into the saddle, then called to Memory, who mewed and launched up to settle in front of him, purring softly as they headed out.

A short distance down the road, two ravens burst from a nearby tree and rose into the sky to fly above him. One cawed out, the sound ringing far and loud in the cold, still morning air. The other was silent, but that was typical of the slightly smaller of the two—Silence, and her chattier sister Song, both dead like Memory. They'd been accidental casualties of one of his first assignments, and he'd been young and reckless enough to try bringing them back, still smugly satisfied with himself for managing so well with Memory only a few months prior.

It wasn't the last time he'd been that cocky, but it was the last time his attempts had been successful. After a few horrific, near-fatal failures, he'd quit making himself pets. Though he couldn't swear he'd behave should something happen to Fury.

The mist cleared away as morning turned to afternoon and came creeping back in as day slowly began to fade to night. He reached the gates of the royal city just as the last of the sun sank beneath the horizon and the call of ghost owls began to fill the night.

"Hold!" called a guard. "Who goes there?"

"Magus Rochus Kraemer, Necromancer of the Queen."

"Hail and good evening, magus," the guard replied and vanished from sight as he called, "Raise the gates!"

The portcullis rose a moment later and Rochus rode through, Memory on his lap, Song and Silence on his shoulders. The streets were largely deserted as he rode through the city. He navigated its twists and turns with familiar ease, for though he did not visit often, he had a sharp memory for such things, a byproduct of all the traveling he did and what he needed to know and be able to recall on a moment for his work.

When he reached the castle, he rode straight to the stables and tended to Fury himself. He left Memory to her hunting with the admonition not to go killing anyone's pets, unimpressed with her obedient mew. Glaring one last time at her, he left with Song and Silence still on his shoulders.

Approaching the keep, he nodded to the guards who pulled the heavy doors open for him and strode into the great hall. Rochus swept his eyes over the hall, across the royal table, but did not see his uncle. Unsurprising, he usually preferred to dine in his room, but it would have been nice to see him on the chance Rochus had to depart immediately to carry out whatever task he was about to be assigned.

Queen Irmhild turned from speaking with the woman to her left, and the frown on her face turned into a pleased smile. "Good, you're here. Took you long enough, magus."

Rochus came to a halt at the foot of the dais and sank to one knee. On his shoulder, Song gave out a short, sharp, echoing caw, eliciting soft whispers and murmurs along the length of the crowded great hall that had fallen silent as his arrival was noticed. "My apologies for the late arrival, Your Majesty. I was far afield when the message arrived."

"Mmm," Irmhild murmured. "No matter, you're here now and no harm done. Rise." When Rochus had stood, she said, "You and your peculiar birds. Did you bring that damnable cat along as well?"

"She goes where I go, Your Majesty."

"See she stays out of my birdhouse, or she'll find herself dead for good, magus."

"She's been admonished, Your Majesty."

Irmhild grunted but did not otherwise reply.

Rochus bit back the questions that wanted out because impatience and rudeness would not get him anywhere. He would know why he was here when Irmhild wanted him to know.

After a few minutes, when conversation had resumed and most had ceased to pay attention to them, the queen finally gave a slight smile and said, "I suppose you would like to know why you're here, magus."

"At Your Majesty's pleasure," Rochus replied.

Irmhild laughed. "I remember when you were not nearly so polite, magus. Of course, I was even ruder than you in those days, hmm?"

Beside her, Consort Gretchen snorted softly. "Was? What is all this past tense?"

"You be quiet," Irmhild said, smile widening. She looked at Gretchen briefly, and kissed her fingers, before finally shifting her attention back to Rochus. "Magus, you have been brought here because I've been called upon to repay a debt and it is not one I can refuse."

Rochus frowned, brow drawing down. "Of course, Majesty, though I confess I'm confused as to how I can be of any help."

"Necromancers are not in great supply, and you are one of only five who fit the requirements—and the only one currently on the continent." She lifted the cup she still held, drained the wine that remained in it, and set it down with a hard clack. "You, my dear magus and old friend, are to be married."

Rochus blinked. Stared at her. On his right shoulder, Song cawed again, startling everyone nearby. "Beg pardon, Majesty?" he said at last.

She laughed. "You are to be married. Lord Landau has called in a favor. He is in want of a spouse and says only a necromancer will do. Given what his family once did for mine, as I said, this is not a request I can refuse. Therefore, you are to marry him — tomorrow."

Rochus was too baffled to feel anything else, though he knew anger would eventually spark to life. "Married. Tomorrow. What is the rush?"

"That is his affair and none of mine," Irmhild replied. "I've had him summoned. You two can talk tonight, and tomorrow morning we'll have the ceremony. It's long past time you were properly settled down anyway, magus. This will be good for you."

And there was the anger, but Rochus tamped down on it with discipline hard won over decades of practice. Landau, Landau... How did he know that name?

Soft footsteps came from behind him and only then did Rochus notice that silence had once more fallen across the great hall. "You called, Your Majesty?"

The voice swept over Rochus like fire and ice all at once, anger and disbelief lodging in his chest and momentarily stealing his ability to breathe. He turned as the man drew even with him and glared at Tilo, who stared back with sad, guilty eyes.

"Well met, my lord," Rochus bit out venomously.

Tilo swallowed, his eyes dimming like a dampened fire. "Well met, magus."

CHAPTER TWO·

After excusing them from dinner, because there was no way he would make it through a tedious royal dinner without finding himself arrested and fined, Rochus led Tilo through the castle to his own rooms. He paid good money to have them retained for his permanent use, but it was a luxury he considered well worthwhile.

He motioned for Tilo to precede him inside, then followed him and closed the door with a sharp, muted bang. Then he kept walking, putting space and the large sofa in the middle of the front room between them. He stared out at the dull lights of the royal city through the window. On his shoulders, Song and Silence shuffled restlessly. "Go, enjoy the night," Rochus said softly. Song cawed and Silence tugged at his hair, then they hopped down to the deep windowsill, fluttered to the edge, and flew off. Rochus pulled down the tapestry to cover the window and keep out most of the chilly night wind.

Slowly turning around, he crossed his arms over his chest and stared at Tilo, who was staring at the floor and looking much like a dog caught stealing supper from the table. "I'm going to assume that last night was no coincidence, though I do not know why you thought it necessary to fuck me before my arrival here. I'd also like to know why I am being made to marry you."

"Because I need a necromancer — "

"Then tell the queen to send one like the rest of the damned kingdom!"

"Don't you think I've tried that?" Tilo demanded, not quite shouting the words, though he may as well have for the fury that filled his voice and blazed in his eyes. "I'm not fucking stupid, nor am I so spoiled a brat or whatever is running through your mind that I thought I must marry a necromancer instead of simply requesting one."

Rochus pressed his lips together. Tilo didn't seem to be lying, but then again, he hadn't seemed to be lying last night either. "Why in the world would the queen refuse your petition? She certainly was amenable to your request for a spouse."

"I've sent ten notices that my lands required the services of a necromancer. Every single time my requests go unanswered. The last one was sent three months ago."

"And upon your arrival? Why come all this way and not ask her directly?" Rochus asked. "Your story melts like ice in spring."

"It's not a fucking story!" Tilo bellowed, all the flames in the room flickering hard in reaction, and a wave of heat washing over Rochus before Tilo tamped down on his dragonfire. "I logged every single one, like I log all such things. I came here with every intention of asking her to send a necromancer and explain why ten petitions for help were ignored. But no one goes directly to the queen about such matters."

Rochus sighed. "No, they don't. They must go through the relevant Supreme."

"Yes, and I did, of course, go to see the Magus Supreme. But his clerks have no record of any of my petitions." Tilo's gaze dropped to the floor, shoulders slumping.

Damn it. One or two petitions might go astray, even three in particularly poorly run territories, given all the steps involved: when a person was troubled, they contacted the lord of the territory, who investigated the matter. If it proved beyond his abilities to resolve, he petitioned the throne for further assistance, either a Queen's Hand if they did not know exactly what was wrong, or a specific type of magi if they did know the exact nature of the problem.

The petitions from the lord were sent to the nearest royal garrison, who would assign the Hand or relevant magi, or send the matter on to the royal castle if they did not have the magi needed. Necromantic matters were rare enough, and necromancers small enough in number, that they were practically never to hand. All petitions for a necromancer invariably went to the royal castle to be handled directly by the Magus Supreme's office.

That ten separate petitions had gotten lost along the way... That most certainly merited suspicion.

"I'm still not following how this provoked you to forcing a marriage," Rochus said.

"It was all I had left," Tilo said, voice thick with bitterness. "I need a necromancer; I have no way of knowing why my petitions are going astray or who is responsible. Every other path available, I have tried. If I went directly to the queen with my complaints, it would take months to sort out, and I've already wasted too much time. This was my only remaining option. I knew her Majesty would not refuse the chance to settle a debt—and nobody could interfere."

Rochus dropped his arms. "I see. So what was last night about?"

Tilo's skin flushed pink, his eyes still on the floor. Rochus suppressed the urge to cross the room and make the little brat look up at him. Licking his lips, looking slowly up then hastily back down, Tilo finally said, "I've never actually met, or even seen, a necromancer. All I knew were the wild stories people like to tell. I didn't want to do something wrong or cause embarrassment, so I went to that tavern because someone said it's a frequent stopping point for travelers and my best chance at finding one. I saw you, decided to chat."

"Chat," Rochus repeated slowly. "You didn't really waste time chatting."

The pink in Tilo's cheeks darkened to red, but he didn't look embarrassed as much as ashamed. The small knot of dread in Rochus's stomach grew larger and sprouted thorns. "You were attractive. I thought, why not see what happens, if…"

"If you could stand to make yourself fuck a half-dead on the chance it was necessary to coax cooperation from your new, reluctant husband,"

Rochus finished.

"That wasn't—"

Rochus didn't want to hear it. "You must have known when you heard my name that I was your intended victim."

Tilo nodded jerkily, more miserable than ever.

"Hoping to entice cooperation before the vows were even spoken?" Rochus spat out, the thorns in his stomach large and sharp, spreading throughout his body, leaving a crushing ache in his chest. Disappointment, regret, and bitterness ran through him like poison. "Whored yourself out to your husband-to-be then disappeared only to leave me feeling the fool upon my arrival here."

"It wasn't—"

Rochus barreled on, refusing to be interrupted by whatever pathetic excuse or justification Tilo contrived. "You forgot one little thing in all your scheming, little kit: all I have to do is marry you. A few vows and some signed papers are all that is required. I'm under no obligation to go anywhere with you."

Tilo jerked, the flush draining from his cheeks, leaving him looking like a man who'd been viciously backhanded by someone he trusted. Tears ran down his cheeks, and the flames in the room went out as a rough, ragged sob echoed through it in the moment before he fled, the door hanging open in his wake.

Leaving Rochus feeling like the cheerless half-dead bastard everyone accused him of being. Tilo was the one forcing a marriage, the one who'd...

Rochus swallowed against the sour scrape of

bile in his throat. Only an hour ago, thinking of Tilo and the night they'd spent together had brought a smile, warmed him as well as any fire. Now he just felt sick, angry enough to slam his fist through a wall. He'd thought the attraction mutual, had thought that perhaps, for once, the goddess was smiling down upon him, or that he'd simply gotten lucky. Instead he'd been the victim of his own damned ego and spent the night fucking somebody who'd never really wanted him. Fucked someone so desperate for help he'd been willing to spread for it.

And instead of acting his age about the situation, Rochus had piled cruelty on top of the whole mess.

He sighed and strode into to his bedroom, stripped off his clothes beside the bed, then washed up at the bowl nearby before crawling beneath the blankets. Across the room, firelight flickered softly, making the shadows dance. Hunger gnawed at Rochus, but he ignored it, too sick at heart to feel like drinking.

There was simply no help for it. He could go to Irmhild and tell her all that Tilo had told him, but clearly the problem in Tilo's territory had been going on long enough. Whatever game was in play, better to deal with the more pressing problem and then sort out the underhanded workings behind it.

And after his recent behavior, the very least he could do was help, instead of fobbing the matter off on Irmhild.

He'd always known he'd be dragged to the

marriage altar eventually. Irmhild was old-fashioned that way, but he'd hoped the situation would be a bit more pleasant than a desperate dragon who thought he had no other options. Fool Rochus for thinking that someone so beautiful, intriguing, and eager would truly want him. The way Tilo had offered up his own blood should have been the first clue; nobody did that. People didn't offer blood unless they wanted something. If Rochus had been thinking clearly—thinking at all—he'd have realized something was wrong. Instead he'd ignored his own advice and listened only to his damned cock.

Tired of unhappy thoughts, Rochus pulled the blankets up high and closed his eyes, counting his breaths until he finally lulled himself to sleep.

Unfortunately, the dawning day was no more pleasant than the night—was indeed a good deal more unpleasant, if the raging storm outside was any sort of omen. Rochus sighed loud and long, then threw open the trunks of clothes he kept at the royal castle and slowly dressed in heavy, formal black robes decorated with silver embroidery depicting the skull and raven crest of the necromancers.

A soft meow greeted him as he entered the front room, and Memory jumped off the couch to come and rub around his ankles. He scooped her up for her morning petting. "Sucking up, hmm? What did you do, kill someone's pet? How many times must I tell you to stop doing that, Mem. How sad would I be if someone killed you for good? Don't do that to other people."

She meowed again then wandered off to go sprawl in the long seat beneath the window she'd long claimed as belonging to her and no one else. From outside came Song's familiar caw, the soft rush of wings. Rochus pulled back the tapestry and stepped back enough the birds could land on the window sill.

When they were settled on his shoulders, he quickly drank the cooled tea on a tray that had been left for him, then ate the cinnamon bread that was also on it as he headed off to get married.

He was directed to the queen's private chapel, where a bleary-eyed priest waited, along with a clerk who was definitely more asleep than awake and looked more than a trifle hungover on top of that. Irmhild herself had dressed just sufficiently enough for propriety; Rochus had every faith the moment the deed was done she would be taking herself straight back to bed.

Tilo stood before the altar, quiet, still, and sad. Everyone around him seemed either uncaring about his obvious misery or was too exhausted to notice.

"It's about time," Irmhild said as she saw Rochus. "All these years and you still cannot be bothered to show up to anything on time, not even your own wedding."

"I show up on time frequently," Rochus replied. "I'm only late to places I don't want to be."

Irmhild rolled her eyes and motioned sharply for the priest to get to work. Rochus sent Song and Silence to the rafters then joined the small party at the altar. A tedious hour later, the vows were spoken and a tattooed band of intricate scrollwork was spelled around the base of Rochus's fingers on his left hand: one for his house, one for Landau's house, one for the church, one for the crown, to represent the bond had been properly and honestly made.

When they were done with the spoken part, it took another hour to go through all the paperwork, and by the time that was finished, all Rochus wanted to do was go back to bed. But he needed blood, and to have additional funds drawn to buy supplies he'd need once arriving at Landau's, and to have a word with a few people to see if he couldn't start piecing together what was going on with the missing petitions.

After the clerk had carried off the paperwork and the priest had quietly slipped away, the queen mumbled final congratulations around a yawn and left, leaving Rochus and Tilo alone.

"I apologize for troubling you, magus," Tilo said. "I hope the marriage causes you no further inconvenience. After suitable time I will, of course, petition for the annulment. Good day — "

"I never said I *wouldn't* come with you," Rochus replied. "Only that it was a flaw in your plan."

Tilo's air of sad resignation turned into ire. "You made your feelings quite clear, magus. Do not act now — "

"I was cruel, I know it, and I am sorry," Rochus said, and though Tilo looked annoyed at the continued interruptions, he remained silent as Rochus continued, "I'll come with you and help with whatever is wrong, and then we'll sort out the matter of the missing petitions. But there are things I need to do here first related to the matter, so is it all right if we leave later this afternoon, at the latest this evening?"

"You'll come?" Tilo asked, looking exhausted and broken and so heartbreakingly hopeful. Damn it.

Rochus gave a bare nod. "With the understanding that you'll annul the marriage after the matter is resolved."

Tilo nodded so enthusiastically Rochus half-thought his neck would snap. He smiled brightly, sweet enough to kiss, and Rochus hated himself. "Of course. I never wanted to force anyone to do anything, I promise. Help me and I'm more than happy to see the marriage is undone."

"Very well, then. I will see you in the main courtyard at the last afternoon cry."

Tilo nodded, then bowed, and Rochus swept out of the room. Song cawed on his shoulder. "Yes, yes," Rochus grumbled. "When I want your unwelcome observations I will seek them out. Until such time, be more like your sister."

He threaded through the castle halls until he reached the Hall of the Magi. Approaching the reception desk in the main offices, he said, "I need to speak with the Magus Supreme on an urgent matter."

"He's quite busy—"

"And the matter is quite urgent, as I said," Rochus cut in. "A matter of necromancy."

The man behind the desk blanched, and

honestly, what kind of idiot was he that it had taken Rochus stating the obvious before he took it seriously? He waited impatiently as the man slipped behind the heavy, ebony double doors that led to the Supreme's private office. After a couple of minutes, the man returned and motioned for Rochus to proceed.

The office was cool and dark when he entered, the door shutting behind him with a soft, muted bang. Incense drifted faintly on the air, sandalwood and a faint burned smell. Song cawed softly on his left shoulder, Silence moving restlessly on his right. Across the room, seated behind an enormous table overburdened with papers, books, and other miscellany, sat a man with thick gray hair and a closely trimmed gray beard. His face was sharply cut, giving him a severe look even when he was pleased about something.

Though at present, he most certainly was not pleased about anything. "What do you want, Rochus?"

"I no longer merit pleasantries?" Rochus drawled.

"They're wasted on you," the Supreme retorted, but the barest hint of smile briefly flickered across his face. "I would have thought a sudden marriage enough to keep anyone busy."

"That is actually related to what I'm doing here," Rochus replied. "Landau—my new husband—claims he's sent ten petitions for a necromancer but none ever came and your office has no record of his requests. Getting sloppy in your old age, Uncle Meyer?"

Meyer snorted. "Yes, but not about my work. We've received no petitions, which means they're going astray long before they reach me. If I were you, I'd have a word with the Megrow offices on your way to your new home—assuming you're traveling with him and not flouncing off back to your tower."

"It's not a tower."

"It's tall, circular, and melodramatic for no reason except to be melodramatic. It's a tower," Meyer retorted, casting Rochus a droll look. "That it's something of a family heirloom does not excuse it from being such."

Rochus rolled his eyes. "Do you know of any reason, magic or otherwise, that anyone would have an interest in Rothenberg Kill?"

Pursing his lips, Meyer leaned back in his seat and clasped his hands in his lap. His eyes were a brilliant spring green, the mark of flora magi. "No current reason," he said at last. "Rothenberg Kill used to have a magi crystal mine, but it was bled dry at least fifty years ago. Whole place sort of faded off after that, people moving on to better places. All that remains is your little dragon and a bunch of dusty farmers, a village or two. His father was no one to trifle with, drove off most everyone. The only one who cares about them is the tax collector. If there's some other reason, and that's related to the lost petitions like you seem to think, I can't imagine what it would be. I think it's just a matter of lazy or stupid magi that I clearly should have been informed about sooner. If that proves to be the case, let me know at once."

"Yes, why waste Hands and money when you can have me do their job for free?" Rochus replied, Song cawing loudly enough to make Meyer flinch. He waved Meyer off when he started to reply. "I'll let you know. Thank you for the help."

Meyer sighed and rose. "I do hope all this turns out well for you, Rochus. Whatever my flippant remarks, I do worry about you out there all alone in my brother's moldering old tower."

"You needn't worry about me," Rochus replied. "I've always been content with my tower and my pets."

"Yes, your little dead miscreants," Meyer said, eyeing Song, who cawed at him again. "I can tell when you're being a smartass, bird, don't think I won't pluck all those feathers of yours and turn them into a hat."

Rochus laughed and gave Meyer a hug as he came around the desk. "I'm sure it would be a handsome hat, but I would not be pleased with you. Take care, Uncle. I'll let you know if anything is amiss with your staff."

"Be careful." Meyer clasped his shoulders, gave him a gentle shake. "And congratulations, I only heard about it a few minutes before I arrived. I was going to come find you shortly. If I'd known sooner I would have attended the ceremony."

"It happened while you were still in bed, so I doubt it," Rochus retorted. "Tell Mother and Father I said hello. Don't mention the marriage: it's going to be annulled the moment this mess is sorted out."

Meyer gave him a look. "No harm in trying to make something of it. You could do worse than a dragon. From what I know of Landau, he's wealthy, hard-working, fiercely loyal… certainly the matter should not have been so crudely forced, but I've seen you do stupider for far less."

"Thanks," Rochus replied, though he couldn't really argue with the truth. "Good day to you, Uncle. I'll visit longer when next I return."

Meyer snorted softly. "I don't believe you, but the thought is appreciated. I mean it about being careful." He hugged Rochus one last time, then walked him to the door and bid him a final farewell.

Next Rochus visited the Office of Records and Deeds to speak with the Land Supreme, Lord Viktor Hoffman, a man all bone and mean little eyes. After Rochus's father had died, when Rochus was still a swaddled babe, many a person had tried to coax his mother into marriage. She had barely a pence to her name, but owned a strip of land that could be extremely valuable in the right hands. Hoffman had, according to his mother, been the least pleasant of those marriage options.

His stepfather had been the most surprising, a lord from a foreign land who'd chosen to leave it after a disastrous marriage of his own and had come to live with his brother Meyer. His parents currently lived all the way to the south on a private island, bought with money his mother had earned after she'd sold her land to the highest bidder and promptly invested it with a ruthlessness no one but his stepfather had apparently anticipated.

"Good day, magus," Hoffman said. "Always a pleasant surprise. How can I help you?"

"Good day," Rochus replied evenly. "I am recently married, as I'm sure you've heard."

Something flickered across Hoffman's face, there and gone too quickly to interpret. Contempt, maybe. "Yes, magus. Congratulations."

"I wanted to learn more about Rothenberg Kill. My husband has rambled about it in that way those who adore something do, but doesn't have much in the way of facts and I'd like to be prepared. My uncle recommended I speak to you."

Hoffman's bored demeanor eased slightly at the mention of Meyer. "Did he? Well, I can hardly disappoint his lordship, but I'm afraid there's not much to tell." His expression turned bland again, but it seemed more contrived this time: his eyes weren't bored at all, but sharp, pensive. "Rothenberg Kill used to be quite the territory back when they were mining magi crystal, but that dried up fifty-seven years ago, and since then it's a forgotten little corner snugged against the foothills of the Creiamore Mountains along the Midwestern edge. Nothing to it but farmland, I believe. Hasn't changed hands in seven generations. I can pull the file if you like."

"No, not at all. I suppose that close to the mountains I should be prepared for more snow than we see here. Thank you for your time, my lord. Good day to you."

"Good day, magus."

Heading off, Rochus visited half a dozen other offices and people, but all told him the same thing: there was no reason for anyone to care about Rothenberg Kill.

In Rochus's experience, when so many people declared something was that boring, it was usually anything but. The question, then, was: what made Rothenberg valuable that nobody was admitting to, or that only a particular somebody or somebodies knew about?

By the time he reached the square at the appointed hour, he was tired, hungry, and frustrated. At least the storm had passed. Song cawed irritably on his shoulder, and Memory was sitting on Fury's back, sprawled across the saddle like she owned it, tail lashing with irritation.

"Yes, yes, we've all had a day that could use improving. Look on the positive side: we're going to a place you've never been, which means there are plenty of victims to fall for your tricks and provide easy prey."

Though that reminded him, he had no idea what he would be doing for his own sustenance. Rothenberg Kill seemed like it would have plenty of farmers, but if Tilo had never seen a necromancer, it was doubtful his tenants had, which meant they weren't going to take kindly to some strange, pale-skinned figure with black teeth asking for them to bleed their animals so he could drink. He pinched his nose, feeling a headache just at the thought of it.

Might be better to buy some animals and bleed

them himself at Tilo's manor. He'd done it before, though he disliked doing it because most animals were nervous around him and weren't inclined to change their minds after he was done with them.

Thoughts of blood and Tilo resurrected memories he'd tried all day to bury, but just like thoughts of fucking him, thoughts of drinking Tilo's blood left him feeling sick, old, and miserable. He really should have known better, but Goddess, what he wouldn't give for that night to have been genuine on both their parts.

He sighed and fussed with Fury's saddle, pausing briefly to pet Memory before he dumped her off it. She yowled at him and swiped at his robes, then flounced off to bathe herself.

As the criers faded off, Tilo came out of the castle and down the steps, looking sad and faded but cautiously hopeful as he saw Rochus.

"Good day," Rochus said levelly. "Shall we be off?"

Tilo nodded and Rochus motioned for Song and Silence to do as they pleased. The ravens pushed off his shoulders and took to the sky. Rochus swung up into Fury's saddle. "Are you shifting? Do you have a horse?" he asked when Tilo simply stood there looking more wretched than ever.

"Shifting, once we're out of the city."

Rochus nodded and held out a hand. "Come on, you can ride behind me, then, else you'll be walking all day."

Tilo stared at him wide-eyed, but after a moment, he slowly took Rochus's hand and swung up behind him. Once he was settled, Memory leapt up and settled in her usual place in front of Rochus. "Thank you, Fury," Rochus murmured, and the unicorn whinnied softly before he started moving, carrying them swiftly away from the castle and through the city.

They traveled in silence, not that there was any way to talk even if he'd been inclined. But it was hard to ignore the warm, thin arms around his waist, the head resting heavy against his back.

Ordinarily he would have kept going, as capable of traveling at night as during the day. He'd only stopped the other night because he'd been in no hurry to reach the royal castle. Now, however, he was hungry, and Tilo would no doubt like food and rest.

Having to stop at the same tavern where they'd met soured what was left of his good mood, but there was no help for it. If they pressed on, they'd have to sleep on the cold ground and would have nothing to eat.

He pulled up to the stable, waited until Memory and Tilo had dismounted, then climbed down himself and handed a coin to the stable boy who came running up. "Come on," he said, casting Tilo the briefest look before turning and heading toward the tavern. "We'll continue on in the morning."

"I—" Tilo swallowed, fell silent.

"What is it?" Rochus asked.

"N-nothing, magus. I'll follow you shortly." Before Rochus could demand an explanation, Tilo turned and fled as though chased by a pack of hungry goblins.

Rochus briefly considered going after him, but the idiot was a grown man and capable of making his own decisions—even extremely stupid ones, as he'd well proven. Leaving him to whatever folly he was about, Rochus headed into the tavern and secured a room, blood, and meal for the night, requesting both be brought to the room.

Once there, he flopped back on the bed and sighed at the ceiling, willing the gnawing worry and guilt in his gut to go away and leave him in peace. He groaned in annoyance when a knock came at the door. At least Tilo had returned. Climbing once more to his feet, Rochus crossed the room and jerked the door open—but the words on his lips froze as he started at a servant rather than Tilo. The girl held out a small slip of paper. "For you, magus. He said no reply was required."

He took the note and handed her a coin, then closed the door and opened it.

I will see you in the morning. Tilo.

Rochus scowled. Crumpling the note, he dropped it on the table next to the tray of food he'd ordered for a frustrating, ungrateful dragon and strode over the window. Throwing it open, he called, "Song, Silence, come to me."

A couple of minutes later the birds flew in and landed on the footboard, flapping their wings, Song cawing softly.

Rochus held one hand out toward them, fingers splayed. Wispy, shimmering gray light spilled from his fingertips and twined around the ravens, whose eyes glowed a deep, rich blue. As the light faded, Silence pushed off the footboard and flew to the arm that Rochus held out. "Find our little dragon, my quiet beauty, share what you see." Silence rubbed her head against his chin then flew off in a rustle of feathers.

Song cawed softly and flew to Rochus's arm as her sister departed. After a few minutes, her eyes began to glow as the spell activated and she saw all that Silence observed. And through Song, his fingers resting gently on her head, Rochus saw as well: Tilo slipping away from the tavern and deep into the woods where he would not be easily found. He settled at the base of an enormous tree, laying out a small, tattered blanket before sitting down and curling up on it, his threadbare cloak pulled tightly around him.

Guilt dropped like stones into Rochus's gut, adding to an ever-growing pile. A lot of things he'd been not seeing, by way of lust or anger, became sharply, painfully apparent. He *had* noticed it when they first met; he'd simply chosen to dismiss it as an exception instead of considering other possibilities.

No two dragons were alike, of course, but dragons as a whole did have a propensity for beautiful, flashy, shiny things. Rare was the dragon not dressed in bright colors embroidered in gold or silver, with enough jewels to make a monarch envious. They adored clothes, art, jewels—all of it.

But since he'd met Tilo, Rochus had not seen him in anything but drab, worn clothes. Even for the wedding Tilo had not been remarkably dressed, and dragons loved special occasions more than they loved fire. A dragon in full regalia could sink a ship, they were so laden with jewels and elaborate clothing.

Nor had Tilo possessed a horse... and it was more than a little strange, of a sudden, that he hadn't been eating in the castle hall when Rochus arrived. But visitors didn't eat for free. It cost Rochus significant coin to retain his room and board there. He'd wager Tilo hadn't been staying in the castle, and that was why it had taken so long to fetch him.

By all accounts, Rothenberg was a wealthy holding. So why was its lord apparently a pauper?

He was also much too thin, now Rochus was paying attention and not thinking with his temper or his dick. He'd seemed healthy, but how much of that was what Rochus had wanted to see? If he'd been in Tilo's situation, he'd have probably resorted to seduction as well.

Letting go of Song, Rochus said, "Silence, guide us to him."

Outside, Song flew into the air, then settled low enough that Rochus could easily follow her once he'd summoned up a small, glowing will-o-the-wisp. Once they reached the trees, Song flew from branch to branch, cawing occasionally, following the silent directions Silence shared with her.

Eventually Silence led them to a small clearing, where Tilo had somehow managed to fall asleep at the base of the tree he'd chosen to huddle up against. "Idiot," Rochus muttered gruffly. He shook Tilo's shoulders, but the dragon only grumbled in his sleep and tipped forward to rest against his chest. Heaving another sigh, Rochus shifted a bit and scooped Tilo up. Still Tilo remained asleep, wonderfully warm but somehow fragile in Rochus's arms. "Lead us to the tavern," he told the ravens, and Song cawed as the ravens took flight.

Rochus followed, the wisp bobbing at his shoulder, the moon lending its own faint beams, until at last they returned to the tavern. Up in their room, Rochus stripped off Tilo's cloak and boots and settled him in the bed.

On the table, the blood he'd ordered had grown cold, though at least it hadn't clotted. He set it by the fire to warm as he made up a bed on the floor, then drank it quickly before bedding down. He was too damned old to be stuck sleeping on floors, but he refused to share a bed with someone who did not really want him anywhere close. If not for the damned mess that had provoked the marriage, Tilo never would have spared him so much as a glance.

And on that depressing thought, he pulled his cloak more firmly around him, closed his eyes, and went to sleep.

CHAPTER THREE

Warm. It was so warm. Rochus might have whimpered ever so slightly. Wasn't strong enough to resist pressing closer to that wonderful heat. It held him close, rumbled something in his ear, and then warm, sweet blood filled his mouth. He swallowed, sucked harder at the source, so hungry for good blood he ached.

A hot, sure hand curled around his hip, a leg sliding over his—and that jolted every lovely thought about feeding and fucking right out of Rochus's head. His eyes snapped open and he stared at Tilo, whose pleased expression turned into one of confusion and alarm.

Rochus jerked away and sat up, hating both of them for the lingering taste of Tilo's sweet blood in his mouth. "In case you've forgotten, we're married and I've agreed to help you. There's no reason to continue whoring yourself out." He stood and left the room, slamming the door behind him. He leaned against it a moment until he could breathe properly and was no longer trembling, then stomped off to the stables to get Fury ready.

Memory was sprawled on the stable floor in front of Fury, who was nudging playfully at her, whinnying whenever Memory took a lazy swipe at him. They stopped when they noticed Rochus, and Memory padded over to rub and nuzzle against his legs. Rochus bent to scoop her up, soothed by her purring as he cuddled her close and stroked her long, thick fur. "A few weeks, months at the worst, and we'll be home again — and pity anyone who tries to make me leave home again anytime soon."

He shouldn't be so angry. So hurt. He hadn't been this upset when he'd been betrayed by lovers he'd known for months and even years. One stupid little dragon shouldn't be so deeply carved into him. It was simply a matter of ego and pride. He'd be over it in a few days.

But even his longest lover had always preferred not to be around when Rochus drank blood. He'd certainly never had a lover who offered it up so easily — so happily, like it never even occurred to them to be bothered. But it *had* bothered Tilo, to the point he had decided he needed a practice run to make certain he wouldn't panic or turn squeamish in front of the man he was forcing into marriage.

That was what bothered Rochus the most in the end. For one fucking night, he'd believed someone had really, truly wanted him, creepiness and all. Not the novelty, not the danger, not the presumed wealth or the fearsome reputation. He hadn't been a malicious dare. He'd just been wanted. He was a necromancer getting on in years, growing colder and scarier by the day, but a young, beautiful dragon had wanted him — wanted him enthusiastically and had been eager to share his blood.

Goddess, he was so fucking stupid sometimes, but he'd give anything for that night, for Tilo's interest, to have been genuine.

Whatever. He would sort out the problems at Rothenberg then put the whole wretched mess behind him as he had so many others. He stared at the tattoos on his fingers, then set Memory down and pulled gloves from an inner pocket of his cloak. Jerking them on, he finally set to work feeding and saddling Fury.

By the time he was done, Tilo had appeared, holding their bags and standing in the stable doorway like he was afraid someone would kick him. "Magus—"

"My name is Rochus and you may as well use it," Rochus snapped. "We're married—it seems stupid to be formal."

Tilo only withered further. "It seems incongruous to be casual when you want nothing to do with me."

Rochus tamped down on the anger that wanted out. He was forty-three years old; he could make some effort to act like it. "The problem is that *you* want nothing to do with *me*, and I am long past tired of being the unwitting assailant."

"I never said—"

"You said enough," Rochus cut in. "Daylight is wasting. We should be on our way." He took hold of Fury's reins and led him out of the stable, then swung up into the saddle and offered a hand to Tilo. "Come on."

"I would prefer to fly, given how unwanted

my company is," Tilo said stiffly. "I'll wait for you at the white trees." He turned and walked out to a clear space, then shimmered and blurred, grew in size, shifted in color until he was a beautiful, dark orange dragon half the size of the stables with a wingspan at least three times greater. He pushed off the ground, took to the sky, and as angry as Rochus was, he still could not deny just how breathtaking a sight Tilo made.

If only, if only. But young, beautiful dragons never settled for old, ugly necromancers, and certainly never in matters of marriage. Not that Rochus was in a hurry to be truly married off. The sooner the annulment took place, the better.

He traveled for three hours without sight of any white trees. All he saw were heavy evergreen trees covered in snow, an icy road, and otherwise a whole lot of nothing. The day was cloudy and dismal, which normally he'd take as a good thing. Though sunlight was not truly a problem for him as superstition said, it did draw unpleasant attention to his appearance.

Memory mewed in his lap, then sat up and growled. Rochus frowned, drew Fury to a halt. High above, Song cawed out, loud and sharp, as she and Silence began to descend.

Rochus felt them before he saw them: wandering dead, freshly dead people brought back to an animalistic version of life, usually by way of a single spirit spread across many bodies. It took a great deal of power, an experienced caster, and willpower strong enough to control them.

As they came out of the trees — at least twenty of the damned things — he could see the silver collars gleaming at their throats. Ordinarily he could have bent enough of them to his will to turn against the others, for he was an old hand with hordes of walking dead, but those collars meant he was locked out.

Why so many? There must be at least fifty of the damned things. Half that number would have been excessive for attacking a single necromancer.

Then realization struck and he felt the fool. Fifty-odd wandering dead was barely enough to take on a necromancer and *dragon*. At full strength, Tilo could have incinerated most of them with little to no trouble; they didn't look old enough to have grown immune to all but shadowfire.

Rochus would have to settle for keeping out of their grasp and finding the person controlling them. He backed further away as they approached, threw out a hand and whispered a spell. Heavy fog poured from his fingers, spilling out to surround him, and then spreading further, hiding the road and surrounding woods, leaving the dead without an easy target since in the fog Rochus would feel and smell much the same as them, and they hadn't looked strong enough to be able to differentiate.

He hoped.

"Fury, off the road," he whispered.

Fury snorted in acknowledgement and rode through the fog like it wasn't there, riding through the thick woods until he drew up to a tree with a wide, heavy branch. Rochus set Memory on it, then climbed up himself. "Go hide — this is going to get worse before it gets better." Fury whinnied in disapproval but rode off. "Song, Silence, Memory, time to go hunting. Find me the one controlling them."

Meowing in satisfaction, Memory licked his hand and leapt neatly down from the tree, vanishing into the thick, swirling fog below. High above him, Song cawed, then the ravens too vanished from sight.

Rochus hated to sit around and do nothing, but someone powerful enough to create and control more than fifty wandering dead was no one to trifle with. Even at his best he'd never managed more than fifteen, and that had left him exhausted and powerless for days. More than likely he was looking for multiple persons, but he should have felt it if so. Such a strong magi presence was nigh impossible to hide.

The real question was: who was behind this and why? They'd clearly been lying in wait for him and Tilo. Whoever it was didn't want them returning to Rothenberg Kill. Why? So many questions, and he was extremely tired of the lack of answers.

From somewhere out in the fog, Memory gave a pained yowl. Rochus's heart seized and lurched, and he threw himself out of the tree without hesitation, whistling for Fury even as he kept running, willing the fog from his path — and nearly running right into the wandering dead coming toward him.

Swearing, Rochus withdrew, called up several will-o-the-wisps, and cast them out to form a circle around him, made them glow with blinding brilliance. The dead circled him, drawing ever closer, and from somewhere in the back, Rochus could hear a smug little chuckle.

"So you're the mighty Magus Rochus. You don't seem terribly impressive."

"I'm certainly going to mightily shove my boot up your ass, especially if you hurt my cat," Rochus retorted, and now he could feel the sharp prickle of holy magic, the purview of priests, healers, and the Queen's Hands—those charged with traveling the land to administer judgment in the far reaches where courts were not available. They also investigated petitions and sometimes helped magi resolve matters, since anything requiring a petition for help usually meant somebody had been breaking laws.

If a Hand was involved in this mess, whatever this mess was, that certainly helped explain why so many petitions had gone astray. It also explained how word had traveled so quickly that Tilo had secured help anyway.

The magi laughed and the sharp tang of holy magic wafted on the air, stirring the wandering dead into a frenzy. Rochus swore, made the wisps glow even brighter though that meant they were too bright for even him to bear. He pulled his dagger and slit his left palm, grimacing at the pain, but there was no help for it—if he was going to survive, there was no time for finesse.

He surged forward, grabbed one of the

wandering dead, and dragged it into the circle of wisps. Then he reached into a pocket, cast down several gleaming white stones, and spoke the words to activate the spell.

"That won't hold for long," the unseen controller of the dead said with a laugh.

Already Rochus could see and feel the ward fraying, unable to withstand the press of so much necromantic power. But hopefully it would hold just long enough.

He knocked the dead he held over, pinned it to the ground, and wrapped his bloody hand around its collar. The holy magic layered upon it burned him, tears of pain streaming down his cheeks, but it was hardly the first time he had been forced to endure the smell of his own burning flesh, so Rochus ignored it.

Instead he poured all his energy into breaking the spell on the collar. But the spell was well-made, had probably taken the efforts of at least two necromancers and the holy magi who'd added the protections afterward.

Just as he was beginning to pass out, he felt the spell break—and all around him the dead rushed in as they finally broke through the ward.

Rochus snarled and took control of them through the broken collar, wresting control from the startled puppet master whose face he still had not seen. The dead went still mere steps from overtaking him. Rochus ordered them back with a sharp gesture, and drove them to their knees. Reaching out through the ether, he found the broken soul used to create the wandering dead and tore it from the bodies, set the soul free.

The bodies collapsed.

Turning toward the source of the only remaining magic, Rochus glared at the shrouded figure walking toward him. "Where's my fucking cat?"

"You're as talented as promised after all," the figure replied, then drew a sword and rushed him, throwing out blinding holy light that worked far too well at rendering Rochus helpless.

He was saved by Song and Silence, who dove and swooped and pecked at the figure and threw him off balance. A moment later, Fury joined the fray, slamming into the bastard and sending him flying into a tree with a sickening crunch.

Rochus could feel him dying. He stalked over to the Hand and knelt, threw back the hood of the man's cloak to reveal a face he didn't know. "What makes Rothenberg Kill worth all this trouble?"

The man spat blood in his face, tried to speak, died with the words gurgling on his lips. Rochus reached out, captured the faintly glimmering spirit as it tried to depart. He beckoned Fury close, stood and extracted a small wooden box from his saddlebags, and drew out the shimmering black crystal within. He whispered softly and the crystal glowed with dark violet light, casting out tendrils that drew the captured spirit into it, then faded once more to a gentle shimmer.

Rochus dropped to the ground, overtaken by exhaustion and dizziness. He looked at his hand, then looked away again, grateful he was long inured to such grisly sights. Way back when he'd first started out, he'd emptied his stomach several times on every assignment. It had taken him months to adjust.

Fury nuzzled anxiously at him, and Rochus reached up with his good hand to pet him. "I'll be all right. We all know I've endured worse. Come on, help me up." Fury turned and Rochus was just able to reach up and grab hold of his saddle. He heaved himself up, swayed slightly, and unthinkingly reached out with his left hand to steady himself.

Agonizing pain shot through him, and with a cry, Rochus blacked out.

He stirred some time later, seeing only darkness, the vague outline of someone leaning over him. Could smell a fire, hear it crackling. He could also hear someone muttering, "You'll be all right, you'll be all right."

Rochus tried to ask who the idiot was trying to reassure, but the words wouldn't form. He was tired. Hungry. So fucking hungry. And colder than he could remember being for a long time. What had happened? He couldn't make his mind work.

The desire to even keep trying skittered away as blood filled his mouth. It was warm, sweet... familiar... Rochus tried to turn away, something nagging at the back of his head, but he still felt bereft when it vanished—and relieved and upset all at once when the wrist he'd been sucking from was replaced by a hot mouth. Fingers tightened in his hair, holding him still as that mouth took his, filling it with blood from a torn lip. Rochus whimpered, kissed harder. He lifted his hand —

"Careful," a voice said gruffly. "Your hand is still in bad shape."

Rochus dragged his eyes open, stared up into Tilo's face, just visible now in the flickering firelight. "What are you doing here?"

"A couple of birds dragged me here," Tilo replied, mouth curving into a brief smile. It fell away as he added, "You were in bad shape when I found you, and you're being particularly stubborn about drinking my blood."

"I don't want it," Rochus said and tried to turn away. He was *tired*. Not from lack of sleep, just depletion of life. Necromancy was draining on a good day, and the combination of battling wandering dead, holy magic, and then capturing a spirit...

He was cold, so cold he ached. The fire was warm, but not nearly as appealing as the body heat still pressed against him, the dragon blood thrumming through his body.

The last time he'd been this miserable after a fight had been five years ago. He'd managed to make it home, thanks largely to his pets, only to find his lover at the time gone, nothing but a fucking note to mark she'd been there at all.

"Let me help," Tilo said.

"Go away," Rochus said, feebly pulling away when Tilo tried to roll him back over. He'd be damned if he let Tilo's guilt and his own weakness persuade him to do something they'd both regret later, no matter how much he ached for it.

Tilo said something rude and colorful enough

that ordinarily Rochus would have laughed. "Stop being a stubborn bastard and let me help. I *want* to help."

"You want to save your home," Rochus bit out. "That's not even close to—" He was cut off as Tilo finally lost patience and yanked hard, forcing Rochus onto his back.

Tilo straddled him, hands braced on either side of Rochus's head. "I know you have it in your head that I'm sacrificing myself or something, but if you'd stop throwing snits and listen to me, you'd find there's not really any sacrificing going on from my perspective."

"I don't—" Rochus broke off with a gasp as Tilo rubbed against him like the evil little bastard he was proving to be, "—don't throw snits."

"Yes, you do," Tilo said. He leaned down, and fresh blood painted his bottom lip as he hovered just out of reach over Rochus's mouth. "Would you trust me to know my own mind? I didn't get here in time to help you when you could have used it, so let me help now."

Rochus surrendered. He'd hate himself for it later, but damn it, he couldn't keep refusing when Tilo kept offering.

Seeing victory, Tilo kissed him, and Rochus moaned at the heat and taste of him, the sweet blood that filled his mouth. Tilo's hands curved around his head, fingers sinking into his hair. Rochus lifted his good hand to curl around him, distantly annoyed that his left hand was still useless.

He frowned when Tilo drew back, but before

he could voice a protest, he was distracted by the baring of all that lovely skin he hadn't for a moment forgotten, though he'd spent hours trying. Naked, seemingly oblivious to the chilly winter air because dragons were brats that way, Tilo once again straddled Rochus. He kissed Rochus hard, leaving his lips pleasantly sore, then began to work his way down the length of Rochus's bare chest, pushing aside the folds of the cloak that had helped keep him warm.

When he reached Rochus's breeches, Tilo opened them and pulled his cock out. Before the chilly air could make Rochus regret his decision, that hot, evil little mouth dropped over it and sucked with truly impressive skill and enthusiasm.

Rochus groaned, fingers twisting in the fabric of the discarded cloak, left hand twitching with the need to do something, his head thumping against the ground. Tilo sucked hard, took him deeper, and Rochus was helpless to do anything but fuck his mouth, thrusting as hard as he could without causing harm, drunk on the blazing eyes that glanced up at him through long lashes.

"Get back here," he snarled when Tilo abruptly pulled off. He finally sat up, but in the next breath forgot what he'd intended to do, ensnared by the sight of Tilo fucking himself on his own fingers, his other hand wrapped around his own cock, eyes making the campfire look dull by comparison as he watched Rochus. He gave a husky laugh, mouth curving in a little smirk. "Brat," Rochus muttered, and pulled away the hand on Tilo's cock to replace it with his own.

He would never admit how much he liked the way Tilo leaned in to him, rested against him as he fought between the pleasure of Rochus's hand and that of his own fingers as he worked his hole open. Eventually Rochus took that over as well, spreading Tilo out on the ground, admiring how decadent and debauched he looked spread on their rumpled cloaks, firelight bathing his sweat-gleaming skin.

When he could take no more of the teasing, Rochus spread Tilo's legs wide and settled between them, lined up his cock, and thrust inside with no warning. He groaned at the tight heat that surrounded him, bracing himself on his good hand, pausing to gather breath. Hot, slender fingers clung to his shoulders, and Tilo's legs wrapped around his hips. "Get to it, magus, or are you so old you've forgotten how it's done?"

"You're not this cocky outside of fucking," Rochus said, but he didn't give Tilo a chance to reply, just did as he was told and got to the fucking.

If there was anything sweeter than fucking Tilo, with the way he clung and begged with those blazing eyes, whispered filthy promises between moans and pants, Rochus didn't want to know about it. He stubbornly ignored every guilty thought nagging at him, that he was just repeating the mistake that had gotten him into this mess to begin with, and pounded into Tilo until he was breathless and sore and couldn't hold back a second more.

He clamped his mouth over Tilo's as he came, shifted enough to get his hand around Tilo's cock to stroke him off, loving the way his body clamped down on Rochus's cock and wrung the last of his orgasm from him.

Rochus collapsed on top of Tilo in a melted, sated heap, breathing heavily, and black spots smearing his vision. He tried to say something, though he wasn't exactly sure what, but before the words could form, exhaustion washed over him and dragged him under.

When he woke again, it was to sunlight and snowfall, though none of it was on him because Tilo had apparently built some sort of shelter for them from branches, leaves, and somebody's cloak.

An annoyed mew drew his attention, and Rochus smiled with happy relief as Memory came limping over to him. He examined her bandaged leg, then whispered a soft spell, lending some of his own strength to speed the healing. "Thank you, beautiful. I'm sorry you were hurt helping me."

She licked his hand and nuzzled his face, then with a flounce of her massively fluffy tail, strutted off to go back to playing with Song and Silence. Fury was nearby under the shelter of an enormous tree, and whinnied softly at him in greeting.

Of a certain dragon, however, there was no sign, though his bags were there, so Rochus assumed Tilo hadn't wandered off too far.

Guilt churned in his gut as the night came back to him, hazy and dull at the edges, but just enough clarity he couldn't avoid just how damned stupid and weak and pathetic he'd been. He couldn't even place a single shred of blame on Tilo this time. It was all him.

Rochus sighed and raked his hair from his face, found his spectacles where they'd been set nearby, then stared down at his poor left hand. Tilo had bandaged it with the same meticulous care he'd bandaged Memory's leg... and how interesting that Memory had allowed it when normally she never let strangers touch her. Rochus looked up and sought out Memory, who stared back at him with her softly glowing eyes and gave a soft, burring mew.

Apparently Tilo possessed a talent for charming dead, spoiled brat cats.

Rochus tried not to think about Tilo's other talents, but he apparently possessed an alarming weakness for young, cocky dragons who seemed eager to fuck him.

Seemed being the important bit, of course, and that withered the good mood he'd almost achieved.

Biting back another sigh, Rochus shoved away the blankets still covering him and hunted out his clothes. By the time he was dressed, he could hear Tilo returning—or someone else approaching the camp, he supposed, but given his pets hadn't so much as stirred, he assumed it was Tilo.

A moment later Tilo appeared, arms full of firewood, cheeks flushed with exertion, eyes as bright and beautiful as ever. Rochus wanted to kiss him, drag him back to their makeshift bed, and see what Tilo looked like when he was fucking Rochus into the ground. But he also wanted to never see the vexing, infuriating bastard ever again, didn't want to desire somebody who only fucked him from necessity and guilt.

The smile on Tilo's face died as he saw Rochus. "Don't tell me you're back to being angry and guilty."

"Says the man who wanted to fuck me because he didn't come flying to my rescue."

For a moment, Rochus half-thought Tilo was going to pitch the wood at his head. "I wanted to fuck you because I wanted to help and because it's not exactly a burden. Believe it or not, I've never had to fake anything regarding you."

"That's not what you—"

"What I say doesn't seem to matter to you!" Tilo bellowed. "You hear whatever lets you stay mad and keep hating me." He dropped the firewood on the ground and turned sharply away. "I'm not saying I don't deserve to be hated, but stop claiming I'm fucking you because I don't have a choice. That isn't remotely true."

Rochus opened his mouth, then snapped it shut again. What was the point? It was done and over with, and he most certainly would not cave to weakness a third time. And the moment the problems with Rothenberg were resolved, he could go home and never think about Tilo again.

He pulled his cloak tightly around his shoulders and went to feed Fury, then spent a few minutes playing with Song and Silence. By the time he was done, his temper was mostly calmed, though he still felt awkward and disconnected whenever he looked at Tilo—who refused to so much as glance in his direction.

Rochus returned to the makeshift shelter and pulled pen and paper from his saddlebags. When he'd finished writing a letter to his uncle, he secured it in a message tube. "Song." The raven flew over to him and held out her right foot. When the message was secured, Rochus stroked her feathers. "Fly swiftly, but be careful. See that no one but my uncle reads it." Song cawed, nibbled at his fingers, then flew off.

"Your uncle?" Tilo asked.

"The Magus Supreme."

Tilo blanched. "Um. I hadn't—I didn't know." He looked like he wasn't quite certain if he was going to throw up, cry, or do both.

Rochus frowned. "What's wrong?"

Laughing bitterly, Tilo replied, "What's wrong? I've forced the hand of the nephew of the Magus Supreme, and if I recall correctly, your parents are nothing to scoff at either. I can't believe I was so stupid, I never registered—"

Standing, Rochus closed the space between them and grabbed Tilo's shoulders, shook him gently. "Calm down before you pass out. If you're afraid there will be some sort of repercussions, set your mind at ease. I'm a grown man. They have no business interfering in my life even if they wanted to, which they don't. My uncle finds all this hilarious and my parents don't even know. When they do find out, they'll join my uncle in laughing at me. Everyone from the queen down is quite assured I'm getting what I deserve."

Instead of laughing as he'd expected, Tilo just looked more wretched. "So I'm both a pathetic, desperate fool incapable of making my own decisions *and* a fitting punishment." He turned sharply away, jerking free of Rochus's hands, but not before Rochus saw the tears.

Before he could catch Tilo again, however, Tilo shifted into his dragon form and flew up into the sky.

"Silence, stay with him," Rochus snapped. "Return to me only after he's made it home safe."

This was *exactly* why he never left his damned tower if he could help it. The only things he excelled at were necromancy and making a mess of everything.

He kicked the abandoned firewood, feeling not remotely better as it tumbled around and into the fire. Putting the fire out, he then turned to breaking down camp. By the time he was done, Tilo was long gone from sight and Rochus suspected he wouldn't be seeing Tilo again anytime soon.

But they had the same destination, and hopefully he wouldn't be further attacked before he reached Rothenberg.

Heaving yet another sigh, he swung into Fury's saddle and rode off after his vanished husband.

Chapter Four

Whatever Rochus had expected upon reaching Rothenberg Kill, it had entailed *something*. Not a whole lot of *nothing*.

The first few abandoned farmhouses had been unusual but not particularly strange, but when he'd reached a village and found it empty — that was strange. When he reached the town that was supposed to be just a couple of hour's south of Rothenberg Castle and found it empty as well…

That wasn't strange, but straight up ominous.

Worse, it looked like everyone had left on purpose. He supposed that was better than a surprise attack that sent everyone fleeing in a panic, or the whole town being dragged off. But it still struck him as worse that an entire territory had packed up and left.

And yet somehow, word never reached the royal castle that something was wrong in Rothenberg Kill. Then again, if the Queen's Hands were involved, even just a few of them, nothing would reach Irmhild if they didn't want it to.

Irmhild was going to burst into flame. Rochus almost wished he'd be there to witness it. Nothing was more hilarious than Irmhild on the warpath — when he wasn't the target, anyway.

He paused at a town board to see if there were

any notices posted about what had happened, but the most recent looking posting was about some pigs available for sale, followed by a yearly feast hosted by Tilo's family that would be taking place two months ago. Forget Irmhild, Rochus was going to start murdering people himself, and if they thought an angry queen was bad, it was only because they'd never seen an angry necro —

A deafening roar made him startle so badly he nearly knocked himself out of the saddle. Fury trembled beneath him, and Song cawed irritably from where she and Silence had perched on top of the board. "That had better not be what I think it is," Rochus said. Because if it was, he was going to well and truly lose his temper and he wouldn't be very sorry about it later.

"Let's go," he said, wheeling Fury around, soothing his trembling with a gentle touch. "Drop me off and you can find somewhere better to be, beautiful."

Fury relaxed under his touch and pressed on, Song and Silence coming to rest on Rochus's shoulders. Memory dropped down to prowl ahead, growling softly as she crept through the high grass.

"There's no way you can kill it yourself — bone wyverns aren't toys!" Rochus shouted after her.

Memory replied with a derisive meow and kept going.

Rochus lifted his eyes to the sky, but he sobered as they crested the hill and looked down in the valley below, where he immediately saw two things:

The sound had indeed been a bone wyvern, which was currently fighting Tilo.

And Tilo was losing. His beautiful sunset orange scales were smeared with blood; his left wing drooped and his right wing dragged.

A bone wyvern: the animated corpse of a giant wyvern. It would take not one but tens, even hundreds, of spirits to bring back a dead giant wyvern if its own spirit was not immediately captured at death. And it wasn't the kind of spirit kept to be useful later, like Rochus had with the Hand's spirit. Anyone willing to endure the difficulty and exhaustion of capturing a wyvern spirit generally needed it immediately — and if the situation was bad enough to require stripping a spirit from a giant wyvern, creating a bone wyvern probably wasn't the solution to the problem.

No, bone wyverns were generally used by posturing twits for purposes of intimidation, destruction, and proving superiority. Usually they were all of the one. The last time he'd seen a bone wyvern he'd been... thirty-two? Something around there. Drunk as a ship full of sailors on leave because he was meant to have been relaxing. Last time he made the mistake of thinking that ever happened.

The damned thing had destroyed three houses before he'd finally sobered up enough to use his magic properly, and he'd been mightily fucking pissed off by the end because getting drunk at all was no easy thing for a necromancer and he'd worked especially damned hard to get shore leave levels of drunk.

And it had all turned out to be the work of some egotistical monster angry with the local justice for daring to arrest him for a list of charges Rochus no longer recalled.

He dismounted, removed his saddlebags, and let Fury run off back toward the village. "Shall we?" he asked his remaining three companions, getting a caw, a flap of wings, and a happy growl in reply. "Let's try a trap, then." Kneeling, he rifled through his saddlebags until he came out with the little wooden box he hadn't touched since putting the Hand's spirit in one of his crystals.

Ignoring the crystals, he pulled out a small velvet bag and tipped out the contents — bone carved into small spheres, etched with necromantic runes for binding, and between them stretched a single spirit so the anchors called to each other and made the trap all the stronger.

He pricked one of his fingers and covered four of the spheres in blood. Sucking on his finger, he gave one sphere each to the Song, Silence, and Memory. "Go." He kept the fourth for himself and tucked the rest away before walking quickly down the hill to where Tilo was barely moving anymore and the bone wyvern was prowling like a predator who knew it had won and was dragging out the thrill of victory. That meant it had been animated long enough the spirits within were merging, become the worst sort of twisted, contorted semblance of life.

Which in turn meant it had been made by a strong necromancer who had intended for the bone wyvern to last, and *that* was a problem of the highest order.

It was also a problem to be dealt with later.

For the present, he went to the spot that would form the northern corner of the trap — a spirit trap, also frequently called a graveyard because people liked thinking they were clever. He felt it when the other three fell into position. He softly whispered the spell, casting out the binding lines between the anchors. When it was nearly done, he looked up and bellowed, "Tilo! Run!"

Tilo, to his credit, went still only for the barest moment from surprise before he moved in a sudden burst of energy, running full tilt toward Rochus. The bone wyvern chased after him, roaring so loudly it resonated through Rochus and made his chest vibrate.

Tilo only just barely managed to stay ahead of it, but that was all the time Rochus needed to close the trap. The bone wyvern crashed against the walls of the trap just as it slammed into place, snarling and screeching — but bound by the will of a necromancer and the power of a captured spirit.

Rochus let out a heavy sigh and fell back in the grass, landing hard on his ass. He took off his spectacles and wiped sweat from his face. "Suck on that, you piece of shit."

A soft, pained whimper drew his attention, and he was abruptly reminded that Tilo was severely injured. "Hold on!" He surged to his feet and back up the hill to his saddlebags, annoyed with himself for not carrying them with him. He tossed stuff as he touched it until he finally reached the small bundle all the way at the bottom: a roll of heavy fabric, at the center of which rested a bottle worth more money than he could count without wincing.

Carrying it down the hill, he cradled Tilo's enormous head as best he could and dumped the contents of the small bottle down his throat. "You'd better keep that down. I don't have another; they're too fucking expensive."

Tilo gave a low, sad rumble, his blazing eye slipping closed. But he was breathing evenly, and after several minutes, his smaller wounds began to close up and the larger ones began very slowly to lessen in severity. Tilo was too big for the potion to work one hundred percent, but it worked enough.

Rochus turned to the ravens and Memory. "Keep an eye on the wyvern. Come get me if something starts to go wrong. Memory, do not go into the trap and fuck with it."

Memory lifted one paw and began to lick it clean.

"I mean it," Rochus said and shoved her head playfully before going back up the hill to gather his things. He slung the saddlebags over one shoulder as he returned to Tilo. "On your feet, you useless dragon. For the record, this is not how you treat a new spouse. You should wait until at least the one year mark to start dragging your spouse into battles and forcing them to use expensive healing potions on your sorry ass." That got him a half-hearted growl, but some of the fire had returned to Tilo's eyes, so Rochus decided to count it a victory. "Can you walk?"

Tilo grumbled again but heaved to his feet. Rochus whistled for Fury, who joined them a few minutes later as they walked along a wide road to the end of the valley and up another hill... to a beautiful, enormous lake. It was so clear he could damn near see to the bottom of it, and so large he couldn't see the other side, just the foothills that framed the far end. The path they walked spilled into a long bridge that led to the castle built in the lake.

"Nothing of interest in Rothenberg, my ass," Rochus muttered. Beyond those foothills were the Creiamore Mountains, which meant the river of the same name. It had enormous value as a travel point through most of the continent, with several tributaries—one of them probably feeding the lake. If it was underground, not much could be done, but if that branch of the river was above ground...

Rothenberg might be a whole lot of nothing, a forgotten territory at the edge of the mountains that divided the continent almost completely in half... but it connected to more important territories, territories that would love to have access to the lake and its connection to the river. It would shave weeks, if not months, off travel time for this corner of the continent. One of those neighboring territories was Morretain, which belonged to Hoffman. How convenient for Hoffman. No wonder the bastard had played so hard at disinterest.

And Tilo had apparently been sitting right in

the middle of it without realizing just how valuable his land was. Or maybe he did know and was acting otherwise.

Mood souring further at the bitter reminder Tilo was a talented liar, Rochus stifled his questions as they continued on across the bridge and through the gates into the castle.

The silence struck him first. A lord returning to his castle should have merited *something*. Tilo didn't strike him as the pomp and circumstance type, but still, someone should have come to greet him. But then, there hadn't been guards at the far end of the bridge either. No one else on the roads.

Was the bone wyvern why everyone was gone? That would make sense, but how could so many people afford to just pack up...

Rochus winced as he realized exactly how they could have afforded it. If a certain stupid, stubborn dragon sacrificed all his worldly goods to save the most precious part of his hoard, moving an entire territory to safer areas would be completely doable.

And then Tilo had gone off and gotten married to someone he could only hope would be able to help.

The idiot seemed to forget that he deserved to be looked after and protected and cared for just as much as everyone else.

Ignoring the bothersome emotions fluttering through him, Rochus pointed at Tilo. "Sit. Do not so much as twitch your tail until you're healthy enough to shift, do you understand me? Is there anyone else around this place?"

Tilo gave him a look and huffed.

"Don't get smart with me — you know damn good and well you can move to answer a question."

Enormous, toothy mouth curving in a way that was unmistakably smirky, Tilo shook his head back and forth.

"No one at all? Idiot. Stay there, I mean it." Rochus turned and swept off up the stairs and into the keep proper.

Like so much else, it was painfully empty, echoing with every footstep, dust already layered over every surface save where Tilo had been coming and going.

It was a beautiful castle, soft white stone on the inside, vines, leaves, and flowers carved right into it along the edges and even completely across some walls. The gleaming wood of the doors, staircase, and the floors was gold-toned and still shiny. He could see the gaps where there'd once been statues, tapestries, rugs, paintings, and other decorative elements. All that remained were plants — scores and scores of plants, more than he could put names to.

He couldn't fathom how breathtaking it would look when everything was back in its rightful place.

It took some searching since the castle was bigger than it looked, and it hadn't looked small, but he finally found a room that looked like it saw regular use. Not the lord's chambers, peculiarly, though perhaps those were simply too big to use when there was no staff to maintain them. The room Tilo seemed to be using was a small space down a quiet hall. It looked more like a room given to a child too big for the nursery, or perhaps an unwanted guest.

He found clothes in the wardrobe and bundled them neatly together before going back downstairs and in search of the kitchens, which proved to be bigger than the entire length and width of his tower. The pantry was depressing by comparison, nothing but bread that looked a couple of days old and cheese that barely looked edible.

Seriously, of what use did Tilo think he would be if he was constantly exhausted and starving? The moment he was healthy again, Rochus was going to strangle him. Or tie him to a bed until he learned how not to be an idiot. "Song, come to me."

By the time he was downstairs and back out in the ward, Song had arrived, perched on Fury's saddle playing with his mane.

After depositing the food and clothes where Tilo could easily get to them once he was able to shift, Rochus went to his saddlebags and quickly wrote out a message. He affixed it to Song's foot, then tied a small bag of coins into Fury's mane.

Song cawed, nibbled at his fingers, and then settled on Fury's head and the two of them headed off.

Hopefully he would get the items he wanted and not wind up robbed, though only a fool dared to cross a magus, especially a necromancer.

He checked Tilo over, smiling faintly that

Megan Den

despite his grumbling he'd fallen fast asleep. Leaving him to his rest, Rochus wandered back into the castle and located a room for himself — large and well-equipped because no way was he living in a damned closet when there were far better options available. He'd already slept on the ground for a month, which was more than enough unpleasant sleeping arrangements.

Depositing his saddlebags at the foot of the bed, he went to figure out the best way to go about a bath. An hour later, he'd settled on just doing everything in the kitchen. There was a tub in one of the storerooms and a large pot to heat the water. That matter sorted, he went upstairs to fetch his soap, razor, and mirror and then went in search of clothes he could borrow since he was long past tired of wearing his own smelly clothes.

Thankfully it took only trying a handful of doors before he found a room that seemed to have been turned into a storage closet for old clothes — his mother did much the same thing, to his stepfather's despair.

Fresh clothes and cleaning supplies gathered, he returned to the kitchen. The hot water felt divine on his skin and after so long with nothing, the familiar lavender scent of his own soap was the best thing he'd smelled in forever. He used a bucket of warm water to rinse everything away and climbed out of the tub before he succumbed to the urge to do a third scrubbing. He dried off his face and hair, then shoved his spectacles back on his nose before pulling on the rest of his clothes.

They were old-fashioned, just the barest bit too small, but they'd suffice until he dealt with laundry on the morrow. He dragged the tub out to drain it, dumped the clothes he'd been wearing inside, and headed back out to the ward.

Which was decidedly lacking in dragon. Rochus frowned. Where had Tilo gone? If the idiot had gone back to deal with the bone wyvern, he was going to wish the wyvern *had* killed him.

The sound of footsteps drew his attention and Rochus whipped around—and stopped short as he saw Tilo standing on the top step cradling a cask of what was probably brandy like it was a baby. "There you are. I thought for a minute you'd gone back to deal with the bone wyvern like the self-sacrificing idiot you are."

"Bone wyvern? Is that what it's called? I'd never seen one before they showed up here."

"*They?*" Rochus's heart felt like it gave out for a beat.

Tilo nodded, casting a glum look at the ground. "Four of them roam around the territory. They never leave it, just stay here, but I've never been able to kill any of them."

"Why not call other dragons for help? Family? Friends?"

"We don't have friends, " Tilo said bitterly. "My father… well, on his good days he was difficult to deal with. On his bad days everyone hid. Plus, I tried and tried to petition for help, wrote letters… You have no idea how hard I've tried to bring in help. But everything was ignored or they showed up wanting to *bargain*." Anger filled his face.

"They'd help if I gave them my land, if I sold them rights to the lake. They'd save lives *only if I gave them something.* So I threw them all out and took care of matters alone."

Rochus made a mental note to get the names of all the greedy, odious bastards later. "I'm sorry. You've done everything right but were betrayed or let down at every turn. For what it's worth, you did choose the right magus for the job. I'm well familiar with bone wyverns and can clear out even four of them, though it'll take me several days."

Tilo looked for a moment like he was going to cry. "Thank you. I know you don't want —"

"I think in the grand scheme of things I have very little to complain about," Rochus interrupted. "Let's take care of the bone wyverns and then we'll sort out everything else. One problem at a time. What is that you're holding?"

"Um. Something that's been in our cellars for almost ten years. My mother bought it when she thought we'd have a necromancer visiting us. I don't remember why now. But the necromancer wound up not coming, and it's a trifle strange for me to sell easily. Then I thought it might be best if I held on to it. For my husband. For you." He walked down the stairs and held it out. "If you want it."

Rochus took it, trying not to gawk like an idiot and failing miserably. "Is this blood wine?" It was more like brandy, actually, but 'blood brandy' sounded strange. Extremely difficult to make, a combination of human blood and brandy, and the northern faeries who made it jealously guarded the secret to making it — which allowed them to charge a damned fortune for it. Rochus had been given a glass of it once in his life and had wanted more for as long as he could remember, but even he didn't make enough money to justify such an expense. Healing potions, yes. Frivolous spirits, no.

Tilo nodded jerkily. "I hope it's good. Um. Did you find a room? I can show you to one of the guest suites — "

"I'm fine, at least until whoever actually has claim to my room returns. You should be resting."

"I just finished resting," Tilo said, though the shadows beneath his eyes and his washed out skin undermined the offended tone. "Thank you for helping me."

"Stop thanking me for doing what I should," Rochus said. "People don't deserve gratitude for not being jerks. I'm sorry about my poor word choice before. I never meant to imply you were a punishment. I was trying to make fun of myself and my hermit-like tendencies."

Tilo nodded and some of the tension eased from his body. "Um. Are you hungry? I can give you my blood, or find something to drain. I think some of the farmers left their herds behind to fend for themselves since it was too difficult to move all of them."

"You're not giving blood until you stop looking one step from death," Rochus snapped, not bothering to say that he wasn't going to take any more of Tilo's blood period. He could still almost taste just how close Tilo had come to dying. If not for the healing potion, he would be dead. "Come on, you're getting more rest whether you like it or not. If you try to argue, keep in mind that I am fully capable of tying you to a bed and not feeling sorry about it."

Something hot flashed through Tilo's eyes for the barest second; if Rochus hadn't been watching so intently he would have missed it. He stubbornly ignored the way his own body thrummed in response. Even if it was appropriate, neither of them was in any condition for such activities.

"I'm not a kit, no matter how much you insist on treating me like one," Tilo replied.

"You are half my age if you are a day and that makes you near enough, especially when you think the best way to help people is by killing yourself!" Rochus snapped.

Tilo's eyes flashed, his hands balling into fists. "I do what's necessary! And you can quit exaggerating. You're not that much older than me."

Rochus wanted to either punch him or fuck him. "You're what, twenty-five?" Tilo's face flushed, and Rochus suddenly didn't want to know the answer. "How old are you?"

"Twenty," Tilo replied, trying to look stubborn but really just pouting. "How old are you?"

When was Rochus going to learn not to start discussions he knew he wouldn't enjoy? He surged up the stairs and past Tilo, calling out, "Forty-three," as he strode into the castle headed for his room. *Fleeing to his room* was more like it.

Twenty, Goddess above. Rochus had thought he was long past making the stupidest mistakes in his life, but clearly he'd just been getting warmed up. And what in the ten hells had Irmhild been thinking, foisting him on some poor, desperate boy in over his fool head?

The sad truth there was that Irmhild hadn't cared. She'd had a chance to rid herself of a troublesome debt and had taken it.

Damn it. Tilo should have friends and family supporting him, looking after him — keeping him from doing stupid things like selling off his entire damned fortune to help people and marrying himself to an unknown person in a desperate bid for help that should never have worked.

Rochus slammed the door of his room shut, set the wine on a table, and crossed the room to drop down on his bed. After a moment he flopped backwards and pressed the heel of his hands to his eyes. How did he get himself into these situations? He sighed and let his hands fall away. The same way *everyone* got into these situations: liking the idea that someone so compelling would actually want someone as uninteresting as him, an obnoxious superior he couldn't defy, and pretty eyes full of sadness and hope.

Still, twenty was a new low. Tilo deserved to have someone closer to his own age at his side, someone he'd connect with, grow with. Not a creepy old necromancer who needed to stay in his tower, orders of the queen be damned.

Heaving a sigh, Rochus sat up and dragged his

saddlebags over, began to pull out everything inside them to put away properly. His necromancy tools went in the chest at the foot of the bed, and the key that had been inside the chest went in his pocket.

The few bits of jewelry he'd brought went in the jewelry case in the wardrobe, the small books went on the table by the bed, and the saddlebags went under the wardrobe.

Now he was officially out of ways to hide away with his shame and mortification. The next time a beautiful, eager dragon climbed into his lap — ha, like that would happen twice in his life — he was going to brain the idiot with the nearest heavy object and run away as fast as possible.

The soft flapping of wings drew his attention and he turned to see an agitated Silence perched on his windowsill. "The one I trapped?" Silence shook her head, flapped her wings again. "One of the others. Impossible to trap with just the two of us, so we'll have to go straight to kill." Then he should probably take care of the one he'd trapped before the necromancer controlling them came to break it free, though Rochus was fairly certain the bastard wouldn't be that stupid. "Come on, then." Silence flew to his shoulder and picked affectionately at his hair.

Reaching up to gently pet her, Rochus gathered his supplies into a satchel, slung it across his chest, and strode off back through the castle to the ward. "What are you still doing here?"

"I wasn't," Tilo said, scowling at him briefly before he turned his gaze back toward the bridge.

"I think one of the bone wyverns is drawing close."

"You're correct." Rochus grabbed his arm and slung him back toward the doors. "You are also staying here."

"You can't make me—"

Rochus whipped around. "Do not test me. There is plenty I can make you do. You are not strong enough yet. You'll do no one any favors by dying pointlessly. I can handle this. You rest, because I will be exhausted when I return and *that* is when I will need you."

Tilo opened his mouth, closed it again.

More gently, Rochus said, "You can't be a good leader if you don't know and acknowledge your own limits. You've done enough. You brought me here to help, so let me help. Keep an eye out for Fury and Song; they should be returning with food and other supplies."

"All right," Tilo said, and Rochus had the impression that if he were in dragon shape his wings would have been drooping. "Be careful."

"That's the plan," Rochus said with a faint smile. Ignoring a stupid impulse to kiss him, Rochus turned and headed out of the castle, off to face a bone wyvern.

CHAPTER FIVE

Getting rid of a bone wyvern entailed emptying the contents, as it were — ripping out all the spirits stuffed inside it. Most of the time that wasn't hard, as they were poorly and hastily made, intended only for show, and the seams easy to tear open and the contents then easily yanked out. Like Memory was fond of doing to his best pillows.

Rothenberg's bone wyverns were not so simple a matter because not only had they been well-made, they'd also lasted a long time, so the various spirits inside had mixed and melded together to become a single, much stronger entity, so that Rochus was less tearing feathers out of a pillow and more yanking an angry bird out of a sack. A large, pointy, violent sack with teeth.

It still wasn't the worst he'd ever faced, though it was probably going to end up an uncomfortably close second. The trick was not using force, a lesson he had learned the hard way.

He was keeping the blood wine, that was for certain.

Silence fluttered on his shoulder, all the warning he had before he abruptly felt the bone wyvern — and a few moments later, heard it down to his bones.

He stepped off the road and into the trees as it came around the bend. Reaching into his satchel, he pulled out a set of panpipes. As the wyvern drew closer he pressed them to his lips and began to play a bittersweet hymn, an old spell that had never translated well to speech. Some spells were simply best cast the old ways.

The bone wyvern slowed, wavered, came to a tenuous halt. Shifted and swayed, stopped and started, caught between the thrall of the music and the original spells driving it. But unlike the necromancer who'd had the sense to collar the walking dead, the necromancer behind the wyverns had trusted solely to his own power and skill.

Whoever was behind this had probably hired the first young, cocky necromancer he'd come across. Or he'd gone abroad for one, though that would have proven more expensive than conniving bastards of this ilk liked. Easier to poach from the young ones who thought being bored was something to complain about and didn't ask questions about what they were hired to do.

Rochus couldn't claim he wasn't stupid, especially given his recent behavior involving a certain beautiful dragon, but he was *old* and stupid, which meant he had a few tricks young fools didn't.

So he played his song and kept the wyvern busy, slowly but surely unraveling the other necromancer's hold. It was exhausting work because he could not stop playing and his energy leeched away with every note, but it was working. And much easier than the flashy way he'd insisted on doing it back when he was young, drunk, and way in over his fool head.

As he felt the wyvern begin to tear, he altered the song to a lullaby, calling to the spirits within, who were drawn to him like dragons to jewels.

Then he felt the jarring *yank* as the other necromancer tried to take back control. The wyvern snarled, but couldn't quite break free of the net Rochus had cast. He played harder, infused the music with even more of his power, ignoring the exhaustion that washed over him.

The other necromancer kept trying, throwing his power like a brawler in a tavern fight. But Rochus had built a wall brick by brick, and it was going to take more than a temper tantrum to knock it down.

When the necromancer was finally forced to withdraw, Rochus finished his song and let the music fade away. Reaching into his satchel, he pulled out the little box that held his crystals and drew out a large black diamond strung on a black thong.

He started humming the lullaby he'd just been playing, letting the crystal sway back and forth. It began to glow as the spirits within stirred and called to those bound within the wyvern.

With a deafening roar, the bone wyvern collapsed, making the ground tremble. As it began to break and shatter and crumble to dust, all the trapped spirits spilled out and drifted toward Rochus's crystal.

As they gathered around him, however, Rochus dropped the crystal, splayed his hands with palms out toward them, and with a few sharply spoken words, banished the spirits once and for all.

They vanished like snuffed candle flames, and Rochus dropped to his knees, trembling with exhaustion and dripping with cold sweat. Silence flapped and fluttered at him, and Rochus mustered a faint smile. "I'll be fine, merely in need of a good night's sleep or six. I should probably take care of that trapped wyvern, hmm? Better two to deal with on the morrow than three." Silence flapped and hopped impatiently. Rochus rolled his eyes as he picked up the dropped crystal and settled it around his neck. "I'll be fine, truly. Stop fussing." She hopped forward and pecked at his hand. "Stop that! No I am not being a hypocrite. I am a long way from a young, idiot dragon who ignores his limits for the sake of saving the world." He jerked his hand away before Silence could peck him again. "Quit your complaining because it won't stop me."

Heaving to his feet, he tucked his dropped box back into the satchel and pulled out the pipes again, along with a small glass vial tucked into a special pouch with three more. Tucking the remainders away, he uncorked the vial and quickly drank the contents — specially preserved pig blood, retained for emergencies. It tasted awful, the spells and herbs used to preserve it ruining the flavor completely, but it gave him a sorely needed boost of strength that should sustain him long enough to take care of a second bone wyvern.

As he climbed a hill and the trapped wyvern came into view, he put the pipes to his lips and once more began to play. The trapped wyvern would be a good deal angrier and more likely to resist than his departed brother, so starting soft and almost beneath its conscious notice would hopefully help Rochus overcome that.

Memory came mewing up as Rochus drew closer, rubbing around his ankles and nearly tripping him in the process. Glaring over the pipes, Rochus kept going. The wyvern snarled and growled when it saw him, fighting the pull of his magic, but also tired from fighting uselessly against the trap.

Rochus increased the volume of his song as he reached the edge of the trap, pouring more energy into it, determined to bend the damned thing to his will.

A sudden sharp hissing, claws in his leg, snapped his concentration like a twig. Rochus looked at Memory, alarmed that she'd do something so reckless, but before he could ask the question, the answer provided itself: two echoing roars, two enormous figures coming over the top of the far hill.

The fucking necromancer had drawn all three remaining beasts together. "Are you serious?" Rochus muttered, stuffing the panpipes back into his satchel even as he turned to run.

Not that he stood a chance of getting away from two bone wyverns, especially given how tired he was, but he wasn't going to stand around and wait quietly for death, either.

The ground trembled and shook as the bone wyverns ran full tilt toward him, their bellows ringing in his ears and thrumming in his chest. Panic drove his feet faster, but it was hopeless. "Silence!" He shouted. "Get Memory to safety!"

Silence obediently snagged the cat and flew off, though it was easier said than done given how much hissing and spitting and fighting Memory did the whole time.

A shadow appeared over Rochus, and he looked up — and could have wept with relief to see Tilo. As he dropped low enough to reach, Rochus jumped and grabbed hold of one his dangling forelegs.

"Not the castle!" Rochus shouted when he saw where Tilo was headed.

Tilo rumbled in annoyance but swerved and flew over a long stretch of trees to what proved to be an old, ivy-covered watch tower. He flew low again and Rochus dropped to the ground with a grunt. Tilo landed next to him and shifted back. Rochus removed his cloak and handed it over; Tilo took it with a murmured thanks.

"Thank you," Rochus said. "How did you know I needed help?"

"I was watching with a bird scope from the gate towers," Tilo said. "I was worried one of the others would show up, or that one would break out of the thing you trapped him in."

Rochus shook his head. "The only way he's getting out of that trap is if I open it or the necromancer controlling the wyverns comes to break it, which they won't because then I'll have the little bastard. The bigger problem is those other two probably still coming after us. At least they won't destroy your beautiful home now, hopefully."

"The castle has withstood worse than this, according to the archives. It's burnt near to the ground twice, at least."

"Well, let's not be in a hurry to make it three all the same," Rochus replied. "Are you all right?"

Tilo shrugged. "Well enough. What do we do?"

"Are you up to fire? I mean a *lot* of fire." Rochus opened his satchel and rifled through it a moment before finally locating the box he wanted. Similar to the other one, it contained several crystals strung on leather cord or occasionally silver chains, but the other box was strictly human spirits. This box contained an assortment of rarer spirits, most of them traded to him — including a large piece of amber that contained the spirits of three dragons.

Tilo hesitated, but then nodded. "Yes. I won't be good for much else after, but I can breathe as much fire as you want. Assuming you don't want me to do it for an hour straight."

Rochus shook his head. "No, merely long enough to burn those two monstrosities to ash."

"They don't burn," Tilo replied, brow furrowing. "I tried that numerous times in the beginning. I swear they just laughed at me."

"We're not going to use dragonfire. We're going to use shadowfire."

Tilo's eyes widened. "I've heard of that! I thought it was just another one of those exaggerated tales people told, like you being half-dead and such."

Rochus's mouth quirked. "Half-spirit is more accurate, though even that's not quite right. And the shadowfire is completely true. It's how I killed a bone wyvern the first time I encountered one." Drunk and scared to death, and the dragon he'd made help him had barely stopped shaking long enough to be of use. "Let's get to a position where they can't get around us."

"This way," Tilo said, and grabbed his hand briefly to drag him along before letting go and darting ahead.

Rochus followed close behind, acutely aware of the warmth lingering on his hand, fighting a sharp need to drag Tilo in close and kiss him deeply.

He really was the world's biggest damn idiot.

Tilo led him to a wall of smooth white rock. "We're in the original kill that gave the territory its name. If we keep going east, we'll come across the old mines. I thought at first that's what everyone was after, but whenever they offered to help, it was in exchange for water rights — if not the whole damned territory, or a marriage contract."

"Goddess have mercy, and people say I'm the half-dead one," Rochus muttered. "Purely to confirm a theory, does your lake have a direct connection to the river?"

"Not until a few years ago," Tilo replied. "I mean, it was always there, but more or less underground. You could follow it through the mountains but only in small boats and if you were willing to risk the currents. But there was an earthquake some years ago that did a lot of damage to the mountains and opened part of the tunnel up. We finished the job because it had become treacherous, so now there's an open path straight on up the tributary. But we don't have much cause to go up that way. It's just a shortcut we use sometimes to trade up north for occasional supplies. Mostly we go south or have what we need here. Is that what everyone is after? A connection to the river?"

Rochus smiled, started to lean in to kiss Tilo before he caught himself. "A direct connection to the river makes your land at least a hundred times more valuable than it was before, and that lake… you could live like a king if you desired, my little kit. Turn your territory into a bustling hub."

Tilo wrinkle his nose. "Why would I do that? I like my territory the way it is, and so do all my people." He slumped abruptly. "At least, I hope they still do. What if none of them come back?"

"They will, and any that don't will be replaced by others. Trust me, there is always someone in want of a home and yours would be perfect for many. You'll have your precious little hoard of people again soon, kit."

Tilo's cheeks flushed. "I'm not a kit."

Rochus just smiled again. "Come on, we'd best focus on the shadowfire and save the discussion of your land for later."

"So what do I do?"

"What dragons do best," Rochus replied. "As they get close, do your level best to set them on fire. I'll take care of the rest."

"Meow."

Rochus looked down at where Memory had appeared from nowhere, a disgruntled Silence riding on her back. "It's about time you showed up, you worthless fur bag. What did you do, stop for a snack?"

Memory meowed again, shook off Silence, and sat back to lick one paw.

Rolling his eyes, Rochus turned his attention back to the matter at hand. "If you think you're in danger of running out of fire, signal somehow, then grab us and fly as far as you can. But even with creatures this well-established, I think we'll manage it. I have very strong spirits here and you're young and robust." The minute he said the words he regretted them—all the more at the brief smirk that curved Tilo's troublesome mouth. "Not a word."

"Not a word," Tilo replied, smirk turning into a full-fledged, mischievous grin. He shrugged off Rochus's cloak and took his time handing it back, making certain it did not obstruct the view.

Pointedly ignoring the view, Rochus dropped his cloak on top of Memory just to hear her squawk of outrage. After she'd managed to extract herself, he pulled out his bag of anchors and gave one each to Silence and Memory. They wouldn't make a truly useful trap, but they could make a wall that'd slow the wyverns down when they tried to escape.

Once Memory and Silence had gone off to take up position, Rochus focused on waking the spirits in his crystal. Beneath them, the ground began to tremble from ponderous footsteps, and the feel of death tingled at the edges of his awareness — and then came the echoing roars.

The wyverns burst from the trees a few minutes later. Tilo shifted, planted his feet, smoke beginning to curl from his nostrils. Rochus stepped well out of his way and called out one of the dragon spirits in his crystal. It was a wispy, glowing orb of dark orange light cupped between his hands, hot and cold all at once.

As the wyverns approached and Tilo spewed fire, Rochus threw the spirit and chanted the spell.

Tilo's flames turned violet-black, and the wyverns screamed as something harmless abruptly turned into something deadly.

"Memory! Silence!" Pulling out the anchor he'd kept for himself, Rochus smeared blood on it, dropped it on the ground, and spoke the spell. A triangle of weak power flared up as the wyverns tried to run. They smashed and smashed against the trap, all the while Tilo bore down on them still breathing fire. As the flames began to turn orange again Rochus threw a new spirit into them.

By the time he had to use the third spirit, one wyvern was gone and the other had not made it far past the broken trap. Though Tilo was clearly flagging, he held up long enough to finish the job.

When the bone wyverns were nothing but enormous piles of ash, Tilo shifted, swayed on his feet, then toppled over and landed on his back on the ground. Rochus walked slowly over to him and sat down with not much more grace.

Rochus meant to stay awake, truly he did, but dizziness and exhaustion rose up like a tide and dragged him under. The last thing he remembered was resting his head on Tilo's stomach.

A dream jerked him awake sometime later, and he glanced around uncomprehendingly for several minutes before puzzling out that he was in his room in the castle. Moonlight slipped through the open windows, and he could just barely see Song and Silence perched on the back of a chair, Memory asleep at the foot of the bed.

Someone groaned softly, and Rochus turned his head to stare at Tilo, fast asleep beside him, stretched out on his stomach, face half-smooshed into his pillow, hair a tangled mess sticking up in every direction. A warm ache that felt entirely too much like fondness curled through Rochus.

The smart thing would be to get far away before he got himself even further tangled in the mess he was in, but he was still tired, and the bed was the most comfortable thing he'd felt in ages, and where would he go in the dead of night?

He settled back down, curled on his side so he could keep staring like a halfwit until sleep pulled him under once more.

When he woke a second time, it was to early morning light. Tilo still slept hard beside him, though at some point he'd shifted close enough to all but wrap himself around Rochus. Carefully extracting himself, Rochus slid out of bed and washed up in the water that Tilo must have left by the fire.

He pulled on more borrowed clothes, gathered up all his dirty laundry in a large basket borrowed from a storage closet, and headed downstairs. Leaving the laundry in the kitchen to attend to shortly, he headed out to the ward where Fury was patiently waiting, enjoying some hay the ravens had probably managed to bring him. Rochus unpacked everything strapped to him, then read the note from the storekeeper that promised everything he'd wanted was there, along with a few other things.

Carrying it all inside, he then took Fury to the stable and got him settled.

Back in the kitchen, Rochus found the large jug of blood he'd requested. He wrinkled his nose at the smell, but it couldn't be helped when blood needed to be preserved for the long term. At least it seemed to have been done by someone who knew their business. He drank three cups then made himself put it away and get to work.

He'd finished the first round of washing and was hanging it up outside to dry when he heard footsteps, and turned to see Tilo, barely dressed in the most ridiculous pair of pants Rochus had ever seen. What was the point of such material, so clingy and loose all at once? They were barely staying on him and yet left very little to the imagination.

"You can do laundry?" Tilo asked around a yawn.

"You make it sound like laundry is as rare and

difficult as necromancy," Rochus said with a snort. "Trust me, laundry is much easier."

Tilo gave him a look. "Most lords I know wouldn't even know where to find the soap; some of them would struggle with the *water*. I certainly can't be trusted with laundry."

"I wasn't born a lord," Rochus replied. "We were quite poor until my mother married my stepfather and sold our land. When I proved to have magus ability, I was sent to school to train but never allowed to forget I was a peasant who wasn't even able to read."

"Oh," Tilo said, cheeks flushing. "I'm sorry, that must have been hard."

Rochus shrugged. "I had the last laugh in the end; they're all deathly afraid now that one day the necromancer they tormented will decide to take revenge for their schoolyard antics."

Tilo laughed.

"There's food in the kitchen if you're hungry, and plenty of it, so help yourself."

The way Tilo's face lit up broke Rochus's heart. He ran off like someone had just offered him a chest of jewels. Rochus stared after him, then shook himself and got back to work. Taking the empty basket with him, he returned to the kitchen, where he was not at all surprised to see how large a dent Tilo had made in the supplies Fury had brought back. "I was going to offer to make a stew for tonight, but at the rate you're going, I'm not certain there will be anything left."

Tilo stopped with a bit of cheese halfway to his mouth. "You can cook?"

"Yes, I can cook. I may not need to eat anymore, but some skills are always useful." Rochus frowned. "Just how long have you been living in an empty castle with little to no food?"

"A few months," Tilo said. "I sent everyone away as quickly as I could once I knew no one would be coming to help us. As soon as everyone was gone I left for the royal castle."

Rochus could think of nothing to say. No, that wasn't true. "You're a good lord." Tilo smiled shyly and looked down at his food. "Though you could stand to remember that you're of no use to anyone if you get yourself killed," Rochus added, unfazed by the scowl that gained him. "Although I suppose that's not true. Such a vibrant spirit would be extremely useful to me."

Tilo narrowed his eyes and slowly stood up, moved around the table.

"It was a—" Rochus oofed as Tilo shoved him backward, butting against the work table behind him, "—jest. I was only jesting."

"Oh, I'm aware, magus," Tilo replied and fisted his hands in Rochus's shirt. "I know for a fact there's more than my spirit that appeals to you."

Rochus again tried to reply, but was cut off by Tilo's mouth against his, hot and insistent, familiar and sorely missed. Damn the man. It took more effort than he'd ever admit to tear away. "What are you doing?"

"What I want," Tilo replied. "As much as you keep insisting otherwise, I've never done anything I didn't want to do."

Rochus tried to shove him away, glaring when

Tilo refused to be budged. "Yes, because if you had happened to be in that tavern on any other night, you would have sought out a crusty old necromancer. I don't understand how you can lie so smoothly in one breath and be so abysmal at it in the next."

"I'm a terrible liar," Tilo said. "Everyone tells me so. I told you, I'd never met a necromancer before. All I knew was gossip. I went that night —"

"To see if you could stand — "

"No!" Tilo said, letting go of his shirt just long enough to thump Rochus on the chest. "Would you let me speak? Not to see if I could stand to go through with anything. To make certain I wouldn't gawk like an idiot or ask stupid or hurtful questions or anything. I was hoping to meet a necromancer to make certain I could act properly and maybe even *impress* you. I got, um, distracted. Then I learned your name and realized I was in trouble no matter what I did."

Rochus kept hold of the hand Tilo had been foolish enough to loose from his shirt and started trying to pry the other one off. "I see."

"No, you don't!" Tilo replied and withdrew — then grabbed him up and slammed him onto the table. Rochus was too stunned to do anything, which gave Tilo plenty of time to climb up on the table, straddle him, and pin his wrists. "You still think I'm lying."

Rochus let out a ragged breath. "In your defense, no one has ever argued quite this... ardently."

Tilo gave a toothy smile. "I'm telling the truth. Do you seriously think I make a habit of approaching men I think won't give me so much as a glance?"

"Habit? I doubt it, as busy as you've been trying to kill yourself," Rochus retorted, "but I find it hard to believe anyone has ever turned you down."

"You tried," Tilo replied.

Rochus sighed. "There are still a lot of old fashioned types around who think necromancers are better off dead, or at least severely maimed. You'd have hardly been the first pretty youth sent to coax me to an unwise location. Let me up, this table isn't comfortable."

"No. Not until you believe me." The scowl on his face looked more like a pout, and despite everything, Rochus almost smiled.

"I believe you," Rochus said. "But whether or not you wanted to fuck me doesn't change the fact that you are *less* than half my age and I am tired—" Tilo cut him off with a kiss. Rochus responded reflexively, unable not to respond to that sweet, hot mouth—but then reality returned, and he bit down hard on Tilo's bottom lip, causing him to jerk back. "Stop it."

"I'm old enough to make my own decisions," Tilo snapped. "If you don't want me, fine, say so and I'll leave you alone. I don't want to fuck somebody not interested in me any more than you do. But it's not your job to make my decisions for me." He scowled harder when Rochus didn't immediately reply, but then the look faltered.

"Unless I misread and you don't — "

Rochus sighed. "This would be so much easier if I didn't."

"So why are you arguing? This is the happiest I've been since this mess started, and it's not every day I get a handsome gentleman in my home and plenty of time to enjoy him."

"Given I'm currently on a *table* in the *kitchen*, I'm a bit concerned about how you want to enjoy me," Rochus drawled, refusing to be pleased by Tilo's words because that was what had gotten him into this mess in the first place.

Tilo grinned, all teeth and triumph. He then ran teeth over the place where Rochus had bitten him and finished the job. The smell of his blood hit Rochus like a wave, and before he could say anything, Tilo's mouth was back on his, eager and determined.

And Rochus just didn't have it in him to keep fighting. "We're not doing this on a kitchen table," he said when he finally managed to pull away. "People cook and eat here."

"This isn't a ploy to get away from me?" Tilo asked.

"No," Rochus said.

Eying him warily, Tilo nevertheless let go of his wrists and climbed off.

Rochus sat up, slid off the table, then stepped in close and curled a hand into the hair at Tilo's nape, drawing him in and lapping lazily at the traces of blood on his lips. Tilo reached up, but Rochus grabbed his hand and pulled it around to curl about his waist. "Slow down, kit. There's no need for urgency here." He lapped at Tilo's lips again, then pushed into his mouth for a long, leisurely kiss that left Tilo trembling against him.

Stepping away, mouth curved in a satisfied smile, he said, "Lead the way."

Cheeks pink, Tilo grumbled something about smug show-offs and brushed past Rochus to lead the way upstairs. He stopped on the landing, however, and dragged Rochus in to press flush against him. "Do that again."

Rochus chuckled and obeyed, cradling Tilo's face and giving him another slow burn kiss, tasting every crevice of his mouth, drawing back to lick and suck at his lips before gently pushing in deep again, over and over until he left them both breathless.

And it was only a kiss, but Tilo already looked half-fucked. His pupils were huge, giving him a dazed look enhanced by the flush that had never really left his cheeks. "I like those kisses."

"Age has its uses," Rochus replied, maybe still a little bit smug.

Tilo rolled his eyes. "You make forty-three sound like ninety-three. And you're a necromancer — even ninety-three isn't terribly remarkable for your kind, right?"

"So they say, but most necromancers die of reasons that have nothing to do with age long before the theory is tested. I'm lucky I've lived this long, honestly."

Tilo made a face and leaned up to kiss him again, hungrier and harder, but Rochus had no complaints. Except that they still weren't anywhere near a bed. Drawing back, ignoring Tilo's protests, he headed the rest of the way upstairs and then through the halls to his bedroom.

Inside, he closed the door and leaned against it, then for once, allowed himself to look his fill.

Tilo stared back at him. "What?"

"You're beautiful."

Face flushing darker than ever, Tilo said, "I'm not remarkable. I look like every other dragon and exactly like my father. Not like—"

"A creepy old necromancer?" Rochus pushed away from the door and prowled toward Tilo all the same, tugging at the laces of his shirt.

"You're unique," Tilo said, splaying his hands across Rochus's chest as he drew close, the word coming out a bit breathless. As always, he was hot to the touch, the warmth sinking into Rochus's chest and spreading through his body. "Everyone says necromancers look like corpses, but you don't, not even a little. I don't understand why people say that. I've seen corpses. You look more like you're carved from pearls and onyx."

Rochus could not remember the last time he'd felt so flustered. Or speechless. He shuddered as those hot hands slipped beneath his shirt and danced across his skin. "It's the teeth that do it, really. People can take me being pale, but the black teeth…"

"They've obviously never met northern dragons, night wolves, or gargoyles," Tilo replied.

"You've met all those but not a necromancer?"

Tilo made a face. "My father tended to only

piss off people he could survive, but they showed up to pick fights frequently. Given how far he had to go to con people..." Tilo shrugged. "I've seen a lot."

"Yes, I suppose you have," Rochus said. "One would think it would improve your problem solving skills."

Tilo narrowed his eyes, then all of a sudden, Rochus was being soundly manhandled again and spread out on the bed much like he'd been on the table several minutes ago. "Just because I must weigh nothing to a dragon doesn't mean you can toss me around—" The words were cut off by an artless but eager kiss, all teeth and tongue and hunger.

Far be it for him to argue. Keep arguing. Whatever. His arms and legs were effectively pinned so Rochus made the most of his mouth. Tilo seemed to have a weakness there anyway. He took back control of the kiss slowly, matching the hungry tone then mellowing it one teasing stroke or nibble at a time, until Tilo was trembling against him and his panting breaths were interspersed with the softest whimpers.

Tilo finally drew back, eyes like a bonfire, and licked his lips. He loosened his grip and Rochus tugged his hands free. He smoothed one hand along Tilo's chest, relishing the heat, the soft skin, the way Tilo moved under his touch. Tilo captured his hand again and leaned in to kiss him.

Blood filled Rochus's mouth, and he drew back with a groan. "You do that like it's the most natural thing in the world."

Tilo frowned slightly. "Do what?"

"Give me your blood," Rochus said, chasing his mouth when Tilo pulled too far away, fisting a hand in his hair and dragging him right back down where he wanted. "That's like the teeth: tends to distress people."

He hadn't thought Tilo's eyes could blaze brighter, but fuck if they didn't turn into an inferno. "I like it. Feels possessive, like you're staking a claim, hoarding something no one else can have."

Rochus ignored how much he liked that idea and settled for more kissing, scowling when Tilo wriggled free a few minutes later but mostly because the wriggling was primarily against his cock.

"Clothes," Tilo said. "Get rid of yours."

"And how am I supposed to do that when I have a dragon on top of me?"

Tilo shifted back and tugged him upright enough to strip off the shirt, then pushed him back down and grinded against him, mouth sucking and kissing along every strip of bare skin he could easily reach.

"Tilo!"

Looking up only long enough to smirk, Tilo began to crawl down Rochus's body, leaving a trail of fire in his wake. Deft fingers unlaced his pants and pushed them away enough to get Rochus's cock out, then that scorching mouth dropped over it and sucked even better than Rochus remembered.

"You're evil. How did I forget how evil you—"

he broke off with a groan as Tilo sucked harder, fingers working into the edge of pants to score and prick with the tips of his claws. He pulled away, causing Rochus to swear loudly. "Get back here."

Tilo laughed. "Patience."

"Shut up," Rochus replied and tried to grab him.

Tilo just laughed and pulled his pants off, cast them aside with the rest of their discarded clothes. "That's better."

"It'll be better still when you get back to work."

"One more moment," Tilo said and retrieved his own pants long enough to pull out the small bottle stowed in them.

Rochus glared at him as he climbed back on the bed. "Did you come downstairs planning this?"

"Yes," Tilo replied and took a long lick of Rochus's cock. "Can I fuck you?"

"I should hope so if you're not going to resume sucking." The look in Tilo's eyes then, Rochus would have agreed to anything. "For someone so impatient earlier, you're certainly taking your time now."

Tilo kissed him, draped across him hot and heavy, giving Rochus plenty to touch. He squirmed away a few minutes later, though, fingers teasing over Rochus's cock before he slicked them and dipped to tease other places. Rochus spread his thighs wide, giving him plenty of room—and swore, nearly coming off the bed, when it abruptly wasn't fingers swiping across his hole. "Tilo—"

That got him a brief husky laugh and then Tilo was right back to it, tongue lapping and then pushing in. Rochus moaned, head pressing hard into his pillow, hand holding tightly to the sheets. The last time someone had done this to him, he'd been young and not a necromancer.

"How did you—" he broke off to moan again as Tilo worked in a finger, "—learn to be so evil?"

Tilo's free hand dug into his thigh, and then he drew back to work in two fingers, mouth wet and gleaming from his efforts. "I told you, we used to get a lot of visitors. Most of them weren't much better than my father; others thought they'd use me as revenge or something. Some were nice, though, and them I was happy to play with and learn from. None of them were like you."

Rochus snorted at that, but didn't reply except to adjust his legs as Tilo withdrew his fingers and slicked his cock. He settled between Rochus's thighs and lined up his cock, then braced himself and slowly pushed in. Rochus pulled him close, dragged his tongue across Tilo's hot, sweaty skin. "Are you a kit or a dragon? Show me what you can do."

Tilo's eyes burned and he growled softly before obeying, pulling out and thrusting back in, making Rochus gasp. "Better, magus?"

"Better, but room for—" Rochus stuttered a broken groan as Tilo slammed into him again, sinking as deep as it was possible to go, hot and hard and the best thing Rochus had felt in more years than he cared to count. He held fast as Tilo continued with the hard, driving pace. If this was how dragons plundered, he was definitely all for it.

At least as long as he didn't think about anything else for too long. But thought was easy to surrender as Rochus happily lost himself in heat and movement and gasping demands for more, until Tilo pounded into him one last time and came with a hoarse cry, fingers gripping so tightly they'd probably leave bruises in Rochus's skin.

Rochus followed a moment later, dragging Tilo close for a wet, sloppy kiss.

They lay in a sweaty heap for several minutes, Rochus in no hurry to be deprived of the warm weight draped across him. Eventually, though, Tilo's weight began to outstrip the warmth, and Rochus finally nudged him. "Come on, as much I would love to lie abed all day, there is work to be done. We have the last bone wyvern to get rid of and then I have to go hunt a necromancer while you put your territory back in order."

Tilo grumbled but obediently sat up, folding his legs in front of him as he stared at Rochus. "I don't even know where to start."

"You start with Her Majesty. Well, no, you take the paperwork you are going to gather and the letter and reports I am going to write to my uncle and he will arrange an emergency petition to the queen. Then you will tell her everything that has transpired over the past several months. It will probably take several months more to bring the matter firmly to a close, but it will finally be done.

You'll not only have your people back, but a good deal more wealth — and you'll never again be in a position where you're forced to desperate straits to save them."

Tilo opened his mouth, but then snapped it shut.

"What?" Rochus asked.

"Nothing," Tilo said and turned to climb out of bed. He retrieved his pants and pulled them back on as he said, "I'll get dressed and meet you downstairs."

He was gone before Rochus could reply. What was that all about? Rochus shook his head. It didn't matter. A few more days and he would be gone hunting the necromancer, and after that he'd be able to head home and put this whole damned mess behind him. Tilo could concentrate on his home and the life he should be living.

Somehow the thought wasn't as cheering as it should have been.

CHAPTER SIX

It took him two months to hunt down and kill the rogue necromancer. He hadn't planned on killing the bastard unless absolutely necessary, but one month into the search, a kill order was delivered via royal falcon, alongside a letter from his uncle confirming Rochus's suspicions that Hoffman was behind it all. He'd gotten further confirmation by way of the necromancer right before he'd followed orders and killed the man. Rochus took no pleasure in killing, but he didn't mind adding the foul necromancer's spirit to his collection.

One month after that, he finally returned to home. The annulment papers came two months later, waiting on his desk when he came home from a trip to the town a few days away for supplies. The thick packet sat on top of a stack of correspondence he nearly pitched into the fire in a fit of temper. Instead, he'd made himself to go bed, and had taken a tonic to ensure he stayed there.

In the morning, he carefully went through every last bit of correspondence before finally facing the annulment papers.

He didn't know why he was so upset. It was exactly what he'd asked for, and Tilo hardly had reason to cling to their farce of a marriage.

Not that he'd know if Tilo felt otherwise; the only word he'd had regarding Tilo since leaving Rothenberg had been whatever his uncle bothered to mention in his letters, and that amounted to very little. Rochus had tried to keep in touch, however pathetic that made him, had sent letters to Tilo whenever he sent reports back to his uncle. The reports received replies. The letters had not. He supposed that was really all there was to say on the matter.

Rochus sent the signed papers out and concentrated on his work, which thankfully turned busier than usual and kept him away from the tower for another three months. Kept him so busy, in fact, he barely had time to notice when the marriage marks faded from his fingers.

By the time he'd returned home again, he'd almost managed to stop thinking about Tilo and wishing there could have been something more than lust between them.

A cool, early autumn breeze drifted through the tower as he settled in his reading room to enjoy a well-earned lazy afternoon. He stretched out on his favorite settee, a book in his hand, a small glass of blood wine at his elbow, and Memory purring at his feet.

Any other day, he would have been happy and relaxed with such an arrangement. Hopefully he would be again soon, and for the present, the book would ideally prove a suitable distraction.

"Magus..." The soft voice of Anel, his housekeeper, drew Rochus's attention. She dipped her head in apology. "I know you weren't to be disturbed, but a strange package arrived with today's post and I thought you'd prefer to see it as soon as possible."

"As always, you're correct," Rochus said with a smile. "Bring it along."

She smiled in reply, then dipped a hasty curtsy before slipping away. A couple of minutes later, she returned, followed by a footman carrying a large, heavy-looking chest. They faded off when he dismissed them, and Rochus stared, confounded, at the large wooden chest sitting in the middle of his reading room.

There was a note affixed to the top, his name written in dark purple ink on expensive, cream colored paper. He broke the wax seal and read the brief message inside: *A gift of courting that hopefully proves my suit is in earnest.*

It wasn't signed, but it also wasn't hard to guess, though *believing* was something else entirely. Gift of courting, was he serious? Just who was the old man here, honestly? Rochus set the note beside him on the floor as he knelt to undo the buckles and flip the trunk open.

Three small casks were nestled inside, stamped with the marks of an expensive winery — one that produced blood wine. A small roll of paper was tucked in the back. Rochus pulled it out and read about the wines enclosed. One was much like the cask he already had, the other two were new vintages ready only in the last year: one with a dragon blood base, another with a faerie blood base. He hadn't known either of those was possible. Excitement and affection rushed through him, and Rochus wished more than anything that Tilo was there so he could express his gratitude.

But courting gift? Really? If he wasn't entirely indifferent to Rochus after all, why ignore his letters? Why say nothing for months except to keep his promise regarding the annulment? Then suddenly this.

No name, though, so he wasn't quite willing to send a note demanding Tilo explain himself.

Rochus called for Anel, bid her see the casks were stored — and the dragon blood one opened.

When he finally tasted it, he both loved and hated it. Everything that reminded him of Tilo was in there, along with the flavors of things he'd not tasted for decades. He was tempted to keep drinking, but he also wanted it to last as long as possible, so once the half-carafe Anel had brought him was gone, Rochus made himself stop for the day.

Try as he might, though, he could not return to his book. The taste of dragon blood lingered, and the note crinkled in his pocket. Curiosity and frustration gnawed at him, and with a soft curse, he finally gave up any attempt at reading and decided to go for a ride.

The next gift came three days later, just as he was beginning to shrug it all off as some sort of jest. It was a velvet box, the kind intended for jewels, large enough it must contain a necklace. He opened the note affixed to it. *Took me longer than expected to get them back, but I was determined.*

The first time I saw you I thought of them.

Rochus frowned, half-afraid to open the box, but he was a grown man and jewels weren't going to hurt him, even if he never felt entirely comfortable wearing them. He flipped the catch and pushed the lid open, and then simply stared.

He thought for a moment they were onyx or black diamonds, but they were sapphires so dark they looked black except where the light struck and drew out the blue. They were oval cut, with delicate black pearls set between them and forming the rest of the necklace.

A beautiful necklace, and it was going to stay exactly where it was because who was he going to impress wearing it? His lazy cat? His housekeeper? Rochus snapped the case shut and gave it to Anel to put in the vault with the rest of his jewelry and other valuables.

Another three days passed before he got the next gift, which proved to be a beautiful new saddle and matching bags, made of black leather and stitched with flowers and birds. "Idiot," he muttered as he traced the impressive stitching. "The third gift is supposed to be given in person." Memory meowed from the settee. "Be quiet." Where was the note? The last two had come with notes.

He checked the box it had all come in, then searched the saddlebags and at last found it.

I wish I could have come, but matters are keeping me here a little longer.

"Hmph." Rochus called Anel and had her fetch someone to take the bags to his room and the saddle to the stable.

The next three days passed with agonizing slowness, but produced a small black box and a note that said only: *As much as I enjoy the thoughts these inspire, the actions will be far better.* Rochus narrowed his eyes and almost put the box away without opening it. But Tilo had his hooks in, damn him, and Rochus finally surrendered to curiosity.

A pretty vial made of red glass held bedroom oil that smelled like night jasmine. There was also soft but strong silk cord and a ring most definitely not meant for a finger. Rochus lifted his eyes to the ceiling, surprised only that Tilo hadn't given such a gift sooner. He shut the box and stored it beneath his bed, but unfortunately out of sight was not out of mind and there were plenty of inspired thoughts to help exhaust him enough to sleep.

Three days later, he wasn't sure whether he should be excited or afraid of the latest gift.

The note attached to the gift said only: *Enjoy.* Rochus opened it, then buried his face in one hand, slamming the box shut with the other before Anel showed up and saw the gleaming artificial phallus within. The mortification that wound through him did nothing to dampen the heat, and despite his best efforts to resist, Rochus ended the night doing exactly as the note had bid, finally falling asleep messy, sated, and hopeful he'd soon see his mischievous little dragon.

Three days later, he was ready to scream, especially when the post had come and gone and there was no new gift. Had something happened? Was Tilo all right? Rochus waited and waited, and finally took himself off to his study to do some work after he snapped at Anel twice.

He'd finally started to get somewhere with his accounting when a sharp rap came at the door. "Yes?" he asked.

Anel's mouth was quirked in a little smile. "Someone to see you, magus."

Rochus's heart began to pound in his chest. "Send them to my reading room. Thank you, Anel."

"Yes, magus." She curtsied and slipped away, and Rochus hastened out of his study and up the curving stairs along the edge of the whole tower to his reading room that took up half the fourth floor.

He ran fingers through his hair, then made a face at himself and dropped his hands, going to the window to stare at the rapidly falling dark. Soft footsteps drew his attention, and all the words he'd been planning and mentally reciting over the past weeks fell away.

If he'd thought Tilo beautiful before, it was nothing compared to seeing him healthy and happy—and dressed like a dragon in a costly green velvet jacket decorated with gold and silver and pearls, more jewels at his fingers, wrists, ears, throat, and even his waist. There was also a small emerald stud in his nose. "You've gotten sparkly, kit," Rochus said, voice softer than he'd meant.

Tilo grinned, pleased and proud. "Bought a lot of it with the money owed me from fines levied by

Her Majesty. She likes fining people, doesn't she?"

"It's her second favorite hobby," Rochus said, then cleared his throat and crossed the room as Tilo did the same. They met in the middle. "What are you doing here? Certainly such a handsome, affluent dragon has better options for courting."

"Shut up, magus," Tilo said, then removed Rochus's spectacles, yanked him close and kissed him soundly.

Rochus had thought he'd known just how much he missed Tilo, but it wasn't until he had Tilo pressed up against him, warm and sweet and achingly familiar, that he realized it ran far deeper than he'd ever realized. He held Tilo tightly, crushing them together, and kissed him back like his life depended on it.

Tilo shuddered, moaned, fingers almost painfully tight in Rochus's hair. Every time Rochus tried to pull away, Tilo chased his mouth and resumed the kissing. He stopped only when Rochus got a hand between them, though he promptly started sucking on Rochus's fingers instead.

"You're a brat," Rochus said. "Why all the gifts? I would have been perfectly happy simply to have a reply to my letters."

Tilo's cheeks turned pink. "I was too scared to read them at first. Your uncle gave them to me, and I put them on my desk to read when I was feeling braver, but then there was so much to do and I was never in my room except to sleep... They got buried and I was worried about so many other things... By the time I remembered them, it

119

felt like it was too late. I read them anyway and realized..." He drifted off, stared at Rochus's chest, fingers tightly gripping his shirt.

"Realized what?"

"I thought you didn't really much like me except when we were in bed," Tilo said. "You were so cold after that last time, and went straight back to business, like maybe the fun was over and it was time to move on. So I tried to act the same. I was afraid your letters would just be more business, more indifference... When I realized they weren't like that at all, I was miserable because I'd accidentally thrown away the chance I'd been hoping for all along." He seemed to droop. "I was sure you definitely hated me by that point, but I wanted to try... did you not like the gifts?"

Rochus brushed a thumb over Tilo's well-kissed lips. "How could I possibly dislike them? And I'm sorry, I never meant to give the impression of indifference. I didn't want to presume or make you feel obligated. You could have the world, Tilo."

"So I've been told, lately," Tilo said, rolling his eyes. He shook his head slightly, then looked at Rochus with an eager smile, his unhappiness vanishing like fog burned away by the sun. "Which gift was your favorite?"

"The saddlebags," Rochus replied, just to see if Tilo would pout, which he did. "Did you really think I was going to name one of your inappropriate gifts?"

"Did you like them?" Tilo asked, eyes going

hot, leaning in close, mouth whispering across Rochus's. "I bought them while I was stuck at the royal castle for months. I'd wander into the city and pick out gifts for people back home. I have an entire trunk of presents for you. It was hard to decide which to send for courting. Oh, except the wine and the sapphires. Those were my first — "

Rochus kissed him, in that slow, deep, thorough way that left Tilo shivering against him and too dazed to do anything but stare and ask for more. "Do you really want a boring old necromancer?"

"You're not boring, and if you don't stop saying you're old I'm going to set you on fire."

"No, you won't, because then you'll never learn whether or not I've enjoyed any of your gifts," Rochus retorted.

Tilo's eyes turned hot again, voice slightly breathless as he asked, "Did you?"

"Now why would I tell you when it's so much more fun to keep you wondering?"

"That's mean."

"So is ignoring me for months and then sending me gift after gift but taking your sweet time coming to see me."

Tilo winced. "I tried to make the gifts worthwhile. They were, weren't they?"

Rochus drew him in and kissed him again, feeling no small amount of smugness at the way it left Tilo clinging and whimpering softly. "What do you think?"

"I think I've really, really missed you," Tilo replied and tried to kiss him again.

"I think you could do with a proper meal, and technically, you owe me a sixth gift. Rude not to show up with one."

Tilo's scowl turned into a grin. "I brought it— sort of. The sixth gift is an invitation to come stay with me for a few months in Rothenberg, see it properly and all. I know you have to work and will get called away, and that you prefer your tower, which is beautiful, but I was hoping—" The rest of his words turned into an indistinct jumble as he happily gave up talking in favor of kissing.

Rochus eventually drew back, but only because kissing was no longer enough. "Come along, my dear kit, I think it's time we take this reunion to more private quarters."

"And you'll come to Rothenberg? It can be weeks instead of months, or just days if you really want—"

"You're quite the talker when you're not half-starved and terrified, aren't you?" Rochus cut in, chuckling when that got him a scowl. "Come on, upstairs." He took Tilo's hand and led him all the way to the top of the tower, where the entire floor was given over to his bedroom and numerous bookcases filled with all the books he'd bought while he was learning to read and after he'd mastered the skill. There was more to the room, but Rochus ignored all of it in favor of leading Tilo to his enormous bed.

Tilo immediately saw the red glass bottle Rochus had carelessly left in plain sight. "I knew it." He turned, grabbed Rochus close, and did one of his damned grab-toss maneuvers. "What else did you use?"

"Shut up," Rochus replied and flipped them over, pinning Tilo to the bed. The image was a thousand times lovelier and hotter in person than it had been in countless imaginings. He drew back enough to strip off their clothes, and that was an even better view. "Lie still."

"That's just mean."

"Call it a well-deserved punishment."

Tilo heaved a sigh but didn't argue. Rochus rewarded him with a soft kiss to those pretty lips before he drew away to make a slow, thorough exploration of Tilo's body with his mouth, starting at the bottom and working his way up, ignoring the hard, leaking cock in favor of leaving wet trails up Tilo's torso and lingering to suck up marks on his beautiful throat.

"Are you going to bite me?" Tilo asked.

Rochus grazed his teeth along Tilo's throat, soaking in the long groan that got him, but didn't bite hard. Tilo might have the strength of a dragon, but his skin was as fragile as any human's and Rochus's teeth were meant for tearing out the throats of his victims.

Tilo whined, high and needy, and Rochus leisurely worked his way back down his body to finally pay attention to his neglected cock, licking along the line of it, fingers caressing, gently squeezing, until Tilo was writhing and swearing and begging.

Withdrawing to slick his fingers, Rochus slipped them back—and moaned to find no preparation was needed. Gleeful triumph shone in Tilo's eyes. Rochus slicked his own cock, then flipped the little brat over, spread him wide, and shoved inside him without warning or care. Tilo growled, thrust back against him, and Rochus fucked him as hard and deep as they'd both been wanting.

When he could feel Tilo trembling, he pulled out and flipped him back over, bent to kiss him hard enough Tilo's lip split. He lapped at the blood, swallowed the shaky moans Tilo fed him, then drew back with an effort and thrust back inside his body, spreading his legs wide and fucking into him with all the strength and energy he had remaining.

Tilo came with a scream, release spilling across their skin, and Rochus gave a last few hard, jerky thrusts before coming himself, Tilo's name on his lips. He collapsed on top of Tilo, took his mouth in a lazy kiss, and then shifted to stretch out alongside him while he slowly calmed down.

"I was worried you wouldn't want to see me," Tilo said softly several minutes later. "I kept waiting in dread for the gifts to be returned, for an angry note telling me to leave you alone."

Rochus shifted to lie on his back, tugging Tilo against his side, head on Rochus's shoulder. He kissed Tilo's brow. "When you didn't reply to my letters, I thought you were done with me. I still think I'm probably too old for you, and many will be more than happy to point that out, but..." He swallowed, held Tilo a bit closer. "I was happy when the first gift arrived, and I know when to stop trying to get rid of a good thing that insists on being in my life."

"Good," Tilo replied and leaned up enough to kiss him hard and quick, leaving Rochus's lips pleasantly throbbing. "Because my backup plan was kidnapping, and I was fairly certain you weren't going to be very amused by that."

"Well, I doubt it would have been worse than a forced marriage and eyes full of reproach," Rochus replied and soothed away Tilo's pout with another kiss. "Rest a bit, then we'll see about dinner and I'll start packing." That earned him a smile and a kiss ardent enough he suspected he wouldn't actually get around to packing for a couple of days.

BOΠUS SHORT

"Get it off me!" The man shrieked in a pitch that normally could only be achieved by boys before their voices changed. "Get it off!"

"Her," Rochus corrected as he crouched to pet Memory, who purred happily but didn't slow where she was licking away the blood from the cut on the man's cheek. "My cat is a lady, and being rude is not going to improve your chances of living. "

The man jerked and yelped, but between Memory and the magic pinning him in place, he wasn't going anywhere.

Rochus stood and removed his glasses, pulling out a cloth to clean them. "Now, then. You have been stealing and selling bodies without the permission of the demised or their surviving loved ones. You have been selling them to people who should not have them. I want a list of all your clients, and every last, single detail you can think of pertaining to them."

"I'm not telling you—"

"You can surrender the information while you live and breathe, or I'll let me cat feast on your brains and pull the information from your spirit," Rochus snapped, shoving his glasses back into place. "Three children have died so far and I intend to resolve this matter before that number climbs. You are guilty of cadaver thieving and aiding and abetting in illegal magic, and I am the one who decides whether it's worth the trouble to send you to court, or if it's better to simply kill you."

"All right!" The man started crying. "I'll tell, I'll tell."

"Memory."

Meowing crankily, Memory took a last few licks of blood and jumped neatly down, going to rub all over Rochus's shins before sauntering off to find something else for dinner.

Rochus broke the spell holding the man in place, grabbed the scruff of his smelly shirt, and hauled the man to his feet. "Start talking."

Shivering and sniffling, the man obeyed.

Two hours later Rochus dropped his off at the nearest royal garrison and, after filling out a report to be sent to the royal castle, decided it was long past time for a meal.

"Magus!"

He paused as he reached the gates, turned back to see a young soldier with the marks of a private on his sleeves. "Yes?"

"Letter for you, magus. Nearly forgot, my apologies."

"Thank you."

"Good night, magus."

"Good night."

Rochus tucked the letter into a pocket of his robe as he headed for the inn he was staying at. In such a large city, he could in theory stay at the garrison — but there were luxuries to an inn, like privacy and quiet and that he wasn't willing to go without.

Once he'd had a hot bath and a pitcher of blood, Rochus settled on his bed and finally took out the letter.

He had expected Tilo's handwriting, some silly letter to make him smile, or to inform him of something that was important, but didn't require haste. Instead, it was in Lele's handwriting — Tilo's steward, and Rochus had never seen anyone command a castle better. Why would she be writing to him?

Well, stupid to wonder when he could easily learn. Breaking the seal, Rochus unfolded the slip of paper and read:

Magus,

A man has come to the castle, claiming to be a friend of yours, by the name of Carsten Bayer. His Lordship was not comfortable turning the man away, but Master Bayer is making his lordship decidedly unhappy. It is not my place to speak for His Lordship, but I worry the man will only grow more unbearable and I know His Lordship would not want to trouble you. I would appreciate your advice on the matter, and apologize if I have overstepped.

Sincerely,
Lele

Rochus snarled at the name. Throwing himself out of bed, he dashed off a quick reply to Lele before packing up all his belongings. "Song, Silence, come to me." He threw open the window, and minutes later the ravens appeared. Fastening the letter to Silence's leg, he said, "Take that to Lele, and watch over Tilo — discreetly, if you please, I don't want him to know. But if that bastard tries to touch or hurt him, do your worst." Song cawed, and Silence flapped her wings, and then they were gone.

Next Rochus arranged for Fury and Memory to make their own way home. "Yes, I know you'd rather come with me," he told a pouting Memory who refused to look at him, putting her back to him as she meticulously bathed one bloody-covered paw. "But you don't like riding on the dragons, and I need to get home in a hurry, so you'll have to suffer. Please keep your murdering to a minimum, there is a hunting limit in these woods and I feel it should apply to you." Memory browed at him and went to jump on Fury's back, where she promptly went to sleep.

Heaving a sigh, Rochus returned to the hunt. The sooner he finished here, the sooner he could go home.

Thankfully, once he found one of the people responsible for the bad spells killing people, that man broke swiftly and the rest were soon rounded up and executed. Once Rochus was certain all their spells and materials had been destroyed, he wrote a final report, recommended a Hand look over the whole matter to be certain he'd missed nothing, and went to meet with the dragon he'd requested Lele send to him.

The dragon, a handsome woman named Antje, smiled as she saw him. Like all dragons, she almost wore more jewelry than clothing, including enormous golden hoops that stood out against her black-brown skin, matched the heavy bands of gold around her neck, arms, wrists, and waist where it peeked out from the long, lavishly embroidered purple tunic. "Greetings, magus."

"Greetings. Thank you for coming to get me. Has anything happened since I received Lele's letter?"

Antje made a face. "Only more of the same."

Rochus didn't bother to ask for specifics. It was Carsten, which meant it was easy enough to guess. "Let's go home."

Beaming, Antje shifted into a large, long and sinuous purple dragon with four glimmering wings. Rochus settled on one of her neck ridges, thighs and hands gripping firmly as she launched into the air. The first couple of times he'd ridden, he'd wound up right back on the ground. Tilo had laughed so hard Rochus had almost quit entirely, not in a hurry to continue humiliating himself.

But Tilo was very, very good at soothing wounded pride and getting himself out of trouble, and Rochus had eventually become a decent rider.

He still preferred keeping his feet on the ground, but sometimes it was damned nice to be home in hours instead of days or weeks.

Especially when he had an unscrupulous ex-lover to murder.

They landed in the castle courtyard, and Rochus had barely dismounted and thanked Antje when a familiar beautiful, vibrant figure came bursting out of the open castle doors and flew across the yard to throw himself in Rochus's arms. "You're home early," Tilo said breathlessly before kissing Rochus hard.

The first time Tilo had greeted him so, it had been a little disconcerting. Rochus was used to a quiet tower and lovers content to wait for him to find them — preferably after washing and feeding. Only Tilo had ever made a production of his returns, and kept doing it over and over and over.

When they finally broke apart, Tilo said, "I thought you'd be gone much longer. Did everything go well, then?"

"As well as it could, all things considered." Rochus frowned as he realized the smudge on Tilo's right cheek was in fact a bruise, like something small and hard had struck him. "Where did this come from?"

"I was helping move some barrels of beer yesterday, slipped and managed to knock my face against an edge. Nothing I haven't done a hundred times, stop scowling."

Rochus relaxed slightly, because Tilo was clearly telling the truth, but not entirely. "Why were you doing that? You have plenty of people to do that sort of thing, and a million duties of your own. There was no reason for you to be hauling heavy barrels up from the cellar."

Tilo's eyes narrowed. "They were short a few people, and my duties aren't that onerous..." Realization filled is face and he bristled like an angry cat. "Someone told you about Carsten, that's why you're home early. I thought I saw Song and Silence last night. Did you send them to look out for me? You of all people should know I can take care of myself." He jerked back a couple of steps when Rochus reached for him.

"You know damn good and well that's not it," Rochus said. "I came home because they said he was making you unhappy, and also I really fucking hate him."

Tilo didn't look much in the way of mollified, but he didn't move away when Rochus closed the space between them once more. "Why in the world did you have an affair with him? And if you hate him so much, why is he here swearing you're friends? I didn't know what to do with him. I thought, maybe you knew something I didn't that made him redeemable, and I didn't want to make you mad by refusing hospitality to your friends."

"It's your home, you can refuse anyone you want. I promise any real friend of mine would have told me they were coming, unless an emergency precluded it, and all of them would understand if you preferred to make them wait elsewhere until I returned. And I don't really have much in the way of friends, you know that. Memory is my best friend, after you."

That got Tilo's ire to drop, and Rochus was treated to an armful of warm and happy dragon. He lingered on a long kiss, nibbling and lapping at Tilo's lips before pushing deeper to taste his sorely missed lover.

"When did you become an exhibitionist, Rochus?"

Tearing away, Rochus shoved Tilo behind him and glared at Carsten, who stood looking smug at the top of the stairs, arms folded across his broad chest, which as usual was covered in a shirt just the slightest bit too tight. He was still handsome, with his tanned skin, pale hair and eyes the green of a lake in summer. The kind of handsome and cocky figure Rochus had found attractive when he was younger and dumber, and now simply found tiresome.

Except... Rochus narrowed his eyes, skin prickling at the presence of magic he hadn't expected. And now he looked closer, Carsten's mouth was too tight and there were faint smudges beneath his eyes, his clothes older than Carsten usually preferred to be seen in. "What are you doing here, Carsten? Besides presuming a friendship that doesn't exist and making everyone here miserable."

Carsten shrugged, face tightening for a moment before settling into a more typical look of careful indifference. "I was in the area on a job and I'd heard rumors you'd taken up with some little dragon boy, had to see it for myself. It's been almost twenty years, Rochus, you can't still be holding a grudge."

"Holding a grudge? Certainly not. You're not worth that kind of effort. But you are still a contemplable, lying, thieving bastard — and that's professionally speaking. Personally speaking, you're all that and much, much worse. It's been seventeen years since we were lovers, but only three years since I had to clean up your mess in Klemens."

Carsten's face soured. "That — "

"If you say it wasn't your fault, I'll let Song and Silence peck out your eyes and let Memory eat your liver from your still-breathing body."

Lips pulling back, Carsten replied, "Of course you still have your little night terrors around. Look, I didn't come to pick a fight, Rochus. I heard tell you'd taken up with him and I couldn't believe it. Not given how pissy you got way back when."

"She was sixteen."

"She was old enough to know her own mind. And you're a fine one to talk, taking up with someone young enough to be your son."

Tilo didn't say anything, but the faint smell of smoke that perpetually clung to him strengthened.

Rochus walked up the stairs and past Carsten, the presence of magic strengthening. Why was Carsten acting like it wasn't there? But he kept walking, replying over his shoulder, "My behavior is not a justification of yours, and there's a world of difference anyway. Go away, Carsten. You're not welcome here."

"I see you still think you're better than everyone else," Carsten retorted. "Some village idiot turned half-dead — "

The rest of what he would have said was drowned out by a roar that sent the few gawkers fleeing for their lives. The next sound to fill the courtyard was Carsten squeaking, and then screaming hysterically, as he was scooped up in Tilo's jaws and dragged into the air. "Rochus! Rochus!"

Rochus went into the castle and headed

quickly for one of the watchtowers. They were seldom used as such, had in fact been filled with couches, chairs, and other old bits of furniture no longer used in the rest of the palace, so people could relax there if so inclined.

He made it all the way to the roof of the west watchtower just in time to see Tilo drop Carsten into the lake—far enough out he'd have an unpleasant time swimming back, but not so far out he'd drown before he reached land. Tilo would probably send somebody to keep an eye on him and make sure of it, anyway.

And once he managed to make it back, Rochus would deal with the real reason Carsten had come to see him.

Tilo watched Carsten just long enough to ensure he surfaced then banked around and returned to the castle. He shifted as he drew close to the tower and landed smoothly on his feet paces from Rochus.

"Been wanting to do that for a while, kit?" Rochus asked with a faint smile.

Shrugging irritably, Tilo said, "I just wanted him to leave. He's been following me like a shadow, and saying all sorts of things." He shrugged again, this time looking uncomfortable. "He never did anything, but it wasn't hard to tell he wanted to, and he clearly thought I was some naïve little idiot who'd like, only slept with one person."

Rochus made a face. "I suppose he thought only an untried, naïve youth could be coaxed into my bed. That's how he likes his lovers, though he's smart enough not to go so young he draws unseemly attention again. I think he only ever took up with me for the novelty, and quickly lost interest. If I could kill or arrest him, I would, but he's always stayed just barely on the right side of the law."

"Well I'll be happy to dump him in lakes whenever I see his stupid face. Especially after all the awful things he said about you."

"What, that you're young enough to be my son? It's true, even if I shudder at the idea of having kids at twenty-three. And half-dead isn't anything I haven't heard a thousand times before."

"That doesn't mean it's all right. You're not half-dead and you're definitely not my father."

Rochus laughed. "That would certainly be a surprise to all of us."

Tilo wrinkled his nose. "An unpleasant one. Please get such an unpleasant thought out of my head."

Stepping in close, Rochus looped his arms around Tilo's shoulders and drew him into a long, slow kiss, the kind that always, even after two years, left Tilo soft and pliant in his arms. "Distraction enough, kit?"

"You're going to have to stop calling me that eventually."

"Maybe," Rochus said, having no intention of doing any such thing, even when Tilo was fifty. He stepped reluctantly away. "I need a bath, and then I will be more than happy to resume distracting you."

Tilo nipped his lips, his throat, fingers skating over Rochus's sides and back. "Or I could help you bathe."

"Or you could help me bathe," Rochus agreed, and went easily as Tilo all but dragged him away through the castle to their room.

The room that was properly Tilo's, the master suite nearly the size of one floor of Rochus's old tower — the tower he'd let a friend use, since he more or less lived with Tilo now, though neither of them had ever really said anything formal about the matter.

It was an enormous room, with a private balcony clearly built with dragons in mind that stretched out over the lake. Rochus loved nothing more than to sit out there and enjoy the view while he read, unless of course Tilo was with him and they talked or behaved rather more lewdly than they should given how easy it was to see them from several other parts of the castle.

There was, in addition to the ridiculously large bed, a fireplace, a large corner filled with sofas and chair, another corner than had been turned into a miniature private library, and small rooms off it for clothes and other storage. Rochus's tower was nothing to sneer at it, but Tilo's home made him feel as though he were living like a prince.

Or at least the grouchy old necromancer sleeping with the prince.

Servants had already prepared a bath, no mean feat given the size of the bathtub, but the castle had some clever little system to send water to the higher floors without having to carry it bucket by bucket. Stripping quickly, Rochus climbed into the water and groaned as the heat began to sink into his skin. It was spring, and warming quickly, but still chilly enough there was nothing better than a hot bath.

Except maybe the warm, slick hands and rough cloth that started to clean him a few minutes later. Rochus dragged his eyes open and drank in the sight of Tilo flushed from steam and exertion, the sleeves of his shirt wet and clinging to his skin. Rochus pushed his hands away long enough to strip the shirt off and cast it to join his own clothes. He curled his fingers into the nape of Tilo's hair and drew him into another kiss. Slick fingers traced up and down his spine, nails dragging occasionally, leaving Rochus shivering.

"This isn't helping you get a bath, though you won't find me complaining," Tilo eventually said, grinning crookedly. "It's good to have you home."

"It's good to be home," Rochus said, and heaved up enough to drag Tilo, pants and all, into the bathtub with him. "I am sorry about Carsten."

Tilo laughed. "I've dealt with his kind before. You forget how loose I was with my favors when my father's associates and enemies came visiting. I was only frustrated because he said he was your friend, and knew so much about you it was hard to call him a liar."

"I'll tell you the names of the precious few I would allow to call me friend, and you won't have to worry about it in the future." He leaned in for another kiss, and frowned when instead Tilo squirmed away and climbed out — but only to remove the last of his clothes before sliding back into the water. Retrieving the dropped washing cloth, he resumed his earlier ministrations.

The tub was a tight, but not unmanageable fit with the two of them, though last time by the end there was more water out of the tub than in it.

This time, Rochus was content to let Tilo wash them both, not certain what he enjoyed more: Tilo's hands all over him, thorough and evil, or watching Tilo wash himself, water and soap all over that fine skin, firelight making it gleam.

He was damned grateful he didn't have to choose.

When they were finally clean and he could not take a second more, Rochus climbed out of the tub and dragged Tilo to the bed, completely uncaring they were still wet.

Tilo rolled them over so Rochus was beneath him, then stared to suck and lick the water remaining on his skin, interspersed with sharp bites that sent shivers up Rochus's spine. By the time his mouth finally dropped over Rochus's cock, it was almost more than he could take. Rochus moaned, one hand clinging to his pillow, the other tangled in Tilo's hair, as he used Tilo's mouth ruthlessly, fucking into it as deep as he could. When he could take no more, he groaned Tilo's name on one last thrust and came.

Looking well-used and pleased with himself, Tilo shifted to straddle Rochus and wrapped a hand around his own cock. Rochus knocked it away and took over, enjoying the heft and heat, the flush to Tilo's skin and the hungry, adoring look on his face.

Tilo bent to kiss, sharp and toothy and flavored of blood, and came moments later in Rochus's arms, making a mess across his skin.

He rolled to the side a few minutes later, and Rochus couldn't muster the energy to get out of bed and clean himself off. He'd probably regret it later, but he was much more interested in falling asleep. With Tilo curled against his side, head on Rochus's shoulder, he did precisely that.

Soft footsteps woke him later, to find the room had gone dark, though someone thankfully had built up the fire — and taken the bath away. How hard had he slept?

Rochus saw someone standing near the bed. "Lele?"

"Sorry to disturb you, magus," Lele said in low tones. Next to Rochus, Tilo remained fast asleep, so warm that he'd kicked off his blankets at some point, though Rochus remained covered. "That man is returning, I thought you would like to know. We've packed his things; they're waiting in the front hall."

"Carry them outside, put them on his horse if he brought one. I suppose put some food with it all. I will deal with him."

"Yes, magus."

Reluctantly climbing out of his warm bed, Rochus went into his dressing room and pulled on breeches, socks and boots, a black shirt, and a mid-weight robe made of purple wool and lined in black silk, a gift from Tilo a few months ago.

He next went to the special set of locked chests

at the back of the room, rifled through the box of crystals in one drawer, picked out a gleaming pendulum carved from jasper. Unlocking another drawer, he pulled out a small black silk bag. Finally he tucked a small bag of coins into a pocket. Pulling the pendulum necklace around his neck, he carried the bag with him downstairs and out to the courtyard.

Pulling the bag open, he tipped out the contents into his right palm and tucked the bag away.

A moment later Carsten came through the gates, soaking wet and clearly pissed. He froze, however, as he saw Rochus. "You fucking bastard! How could you let him — "

"I let him do nothing," Rochus said. "Young or not, he's an adult, and if you make him angry in his own damned castle, Carsten, you have no one but yourself to blame for the consequences. Why did you really come here?"

Carsten's mouth flattened. "Like I said, everybody was talking about how you were living with some kid and having a grand old time. I couldn't believe it, not with how sanctimonious you got with me. There's a lot more years between the two of you than there ever was between me and that girl. I thought you'd finally loosened up."

"Out of friends and in need of a favor?"

"Fuck you, Rochus. Always acting like you're better than all of us, living in your tower and letting no one in unless it's to warm your bed. The snotty necromancer pet of the queen. Is that what he sees in you?"

Rochus shook his head, saying nothing as he heard Lele and a few others come up behind him. They set the bags containing Carsten's belongings a few paces in front of Rochus when he motioned. On top of the pile Rochus threw the sack of coins he'd brought with him. Then he let the long, slippery, thread-thin string in his left handle tumble down, and looped it over each of his middle fingers. A few softly whispered words of magic and the pendulum around his neck began to glow. "Lele, did you or anyone else happen to see a Hands uniform in those bags?"

But the sour, bitter look on Carsten's face was all the answer he needed.

Lele replied, "I packed everything myself. There was no uniform."

"As I thought, and instead of coming here and asking me for help, and treating my lover and his people kindly, you behave like a jealous, bitter bastard," Rochus said. "Once upon a time, I might have hit you for that."

Carsten sneered. "Fuck you."

"Lele, you and the others can return. Go to bed. I'll tend the rest of this."

"Yes, magus."

When they'd gone, Rochus touched the glowing jasper with his right hand and drew out a thin strand of the spirit inside — the spirit of an ichor spider, brown-red and viscous, as sticky and poisonous as the webs it had once spun in life. "There's money enough there to live well for a year if you're smart about, Carsten. Food for days and knowing Lele, additional supplies that should keep you well for some time. More than you deserve, given how rotten you are to everyone you cross." Carsten opened his mouth, but shut it again.

Humming softly, Rochus began to weave the long loop of string between his fingers, twisting and turning it, all the while weaving the spider's soul with it, until he spread between his fingers an intricate web saturated and sticky with poisonous soul.

Across the courtyard, Carsten had dropped to his knees and was clutching at his chest, panting heavily.

With a last few notes, the web vanished, and Carsten toppled over with a cry.

Rochus walked over to him, and as he stopped Song and Silence came swooping down from the sky to settle on his shoulders. Song's caw echoed across the courtyard.

Carsten glared up at him. "Cursing is illegal, you blood-drinking bastard. And your magic is for dead things."

"It's not a curse," Rochus replied. "Stop treating me like an idiot, Carsten. You clearly came to me for help — why not just *say* that. I don't like you anymore, but I would have helped you. *Have* helped you."

Carsten's frown cut deeply into his face as he sat up and scowled at the stones of the courtyard.

Rochus sighed. "My magic is for dead things — and things cursed by necromancy. Who did you piss off that put a spirit drain in you?"

"I don't know," Carsten said, sounding exhausted and three times his age. "I woke up two weeks ago and felt sick. Couldn't keep anything on my stomach for days, and even now, I have to be careful. A healer told me I'd been death-cursed, but she didn't know more than that. Told me to find a necromancer and to do it quickly. I'd heard you were in this area, so I came here… and I don't know. I was angry."

"Well you're going to feel like death for a few days while the ichor poison works. It can't kill you, but it is one of the few things that can break a spirit drain—and kill the source. Once that curse is broken and the necromancer is dead, you'll be fine again. I would say about six days, but possibly as many as eight. I suggest you make your way to a garrison and tell them what is happening. They can keep an eye on you, and once the curse is taken care of can ensure you're seen by a healer." He sighed again. "You know, if you'd shown up and apologized and been decent, this could have gone differently. We'll never be friends again, but we would have treated you well."

Carsten stood, weary and defeated. "Just… leave me alone, Rochus. I'm grateful you helped me, I really am, but leave me alone." He gathered up his belongings, including the sack of coins, and left without a backward glance.

When he was well out of sight and the guards dropped the portcullis, Rochus turned to go back inside.

He wasn't remotely surprised to see Tilo standing on the stairs. "What's going on?"

"He came for help, and as per usual, proved too proud and stubborn and scared to simply ask for it. Someone he pissed off had a soul drain put on him." At Tilo's questioning look, he said, "Some living souls are weaker than others, usually from a hard life or, like Carsten, being a bastard. It means they're susceptible to necromancy, the same way a weakened body is more susceptible to illness. A soul drain is a curse that drains the soul drop by drop, usually over the course of weeks, though it can be done in days or dragged out for months. It's already been two for Carsten; another four and he'd be dead."

"So he came here and acted like an ass?"

"I think he doesn't know any other way to be, and fell back on bad habits," Rochus replied.

"He'll be all right now?" Tilo asked.

Rochus shrugged. "He'll be safe from the soul drain. I can't speak to what anyone else might do to him."

Tilo took his hand and drew him close. "I'm glad you were able to help him. Nobody deserves to die like that." He leaned up and kissed Rochus softly. "You've yet to feed properly, magus. I'm sure you're even hungrier after casting a spell like that. Come to bed and have a drink."

"If you insist," Rochus replied, and kept hold of his hand as they vanished into the castle.

About the Author

Megan is a long time resident of LGBTQ romance, and keeps herself busy reading, writing, and publishing it. She is often accused of fluff and nonsense. When she's not involved in writing, she likes to cook, harass her cats, or watch movies. She loves to hear from readers, and can be found all over the internet.

maderr.com
maderr.tumblr.com
meganaderr.blogspot.com
facebook.com/meganaprilderr
meganaderr@gmail.com
@meganaderr